Stitch

Woody

Baloo

Rapunzel

Nick

Cinderella

Jessie

Goofy

Ariel

Lilo

Mulan

Sulley

Nemo

Elsa

Nala

Lightning McQueen

*mermaid*

*fish*

First published in the UK by Autumn Publishing in 2022,
an imprint of Bonnier Books UK.
Published by Scholastic Australia in 2022.



0322 001
ISBN 978-1-76120-474-6

Printed and manufactured in China.

10 9 8 7 6 5 4 3 2 1 22 23 24 25 26 / 2

*lion cub*

*toy*

*ukulele*

# MY FIRST DISNEY 1000 WORDS

SCHOLASTIC

# Dear Parent,

Welcome to Disney Learning's **My First 1000 Words.** This book, filled with beautiful illustrations of more than a thousand words, is designed to help young learners develop a rich, substantial vocabulary. Research shows that vocabulary is an accurate predictor of later literacy skills and school success. Acquiring the language to describe the world around them empowers children to express their observations, thoughts and feelings.

Beloved Disney characters accompany your child on this journey through the wonderful world of words. The words in this book are organised into five engaging content areas. Each section presents a variety of thematically related scenes intended to spark curiosity, imagination and conversation. Talk about the words and pictures in this book together. Encourage your child to point out details, ask questions and tell stories about what's on the page. Sharing this book can be a fun, meaningful family experience.

We hope this book provides an enjoyable step on your child's road to becoming a confident reader. Turn the page, and let's get started!

# Contents

HOME and
FAMILY

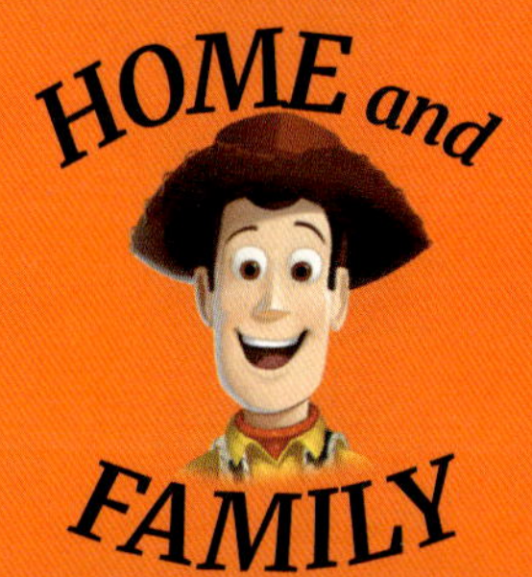

# Woody and Friends Play in the Garden

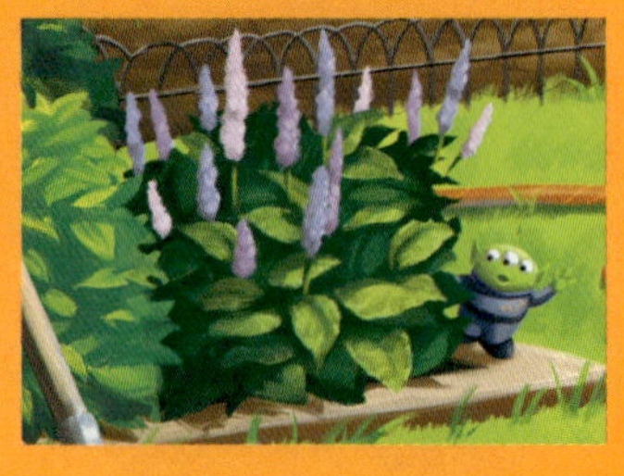

flower bed

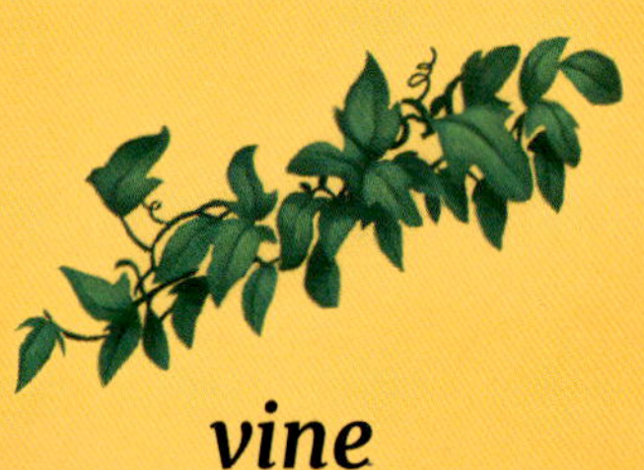

vine

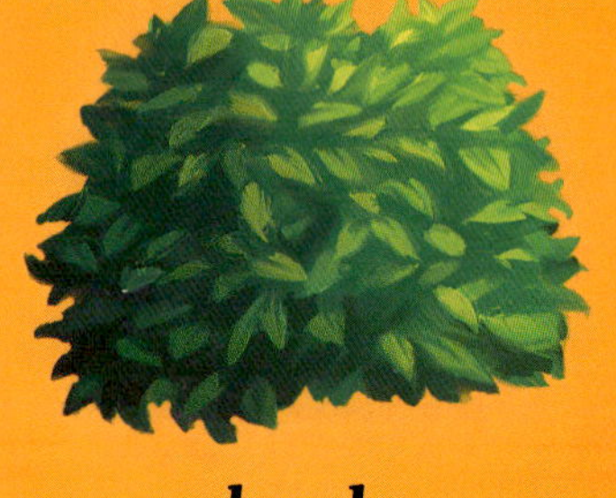

bush

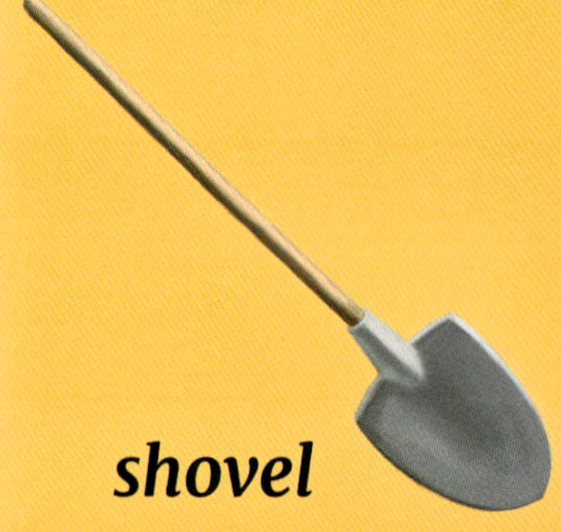

shovel

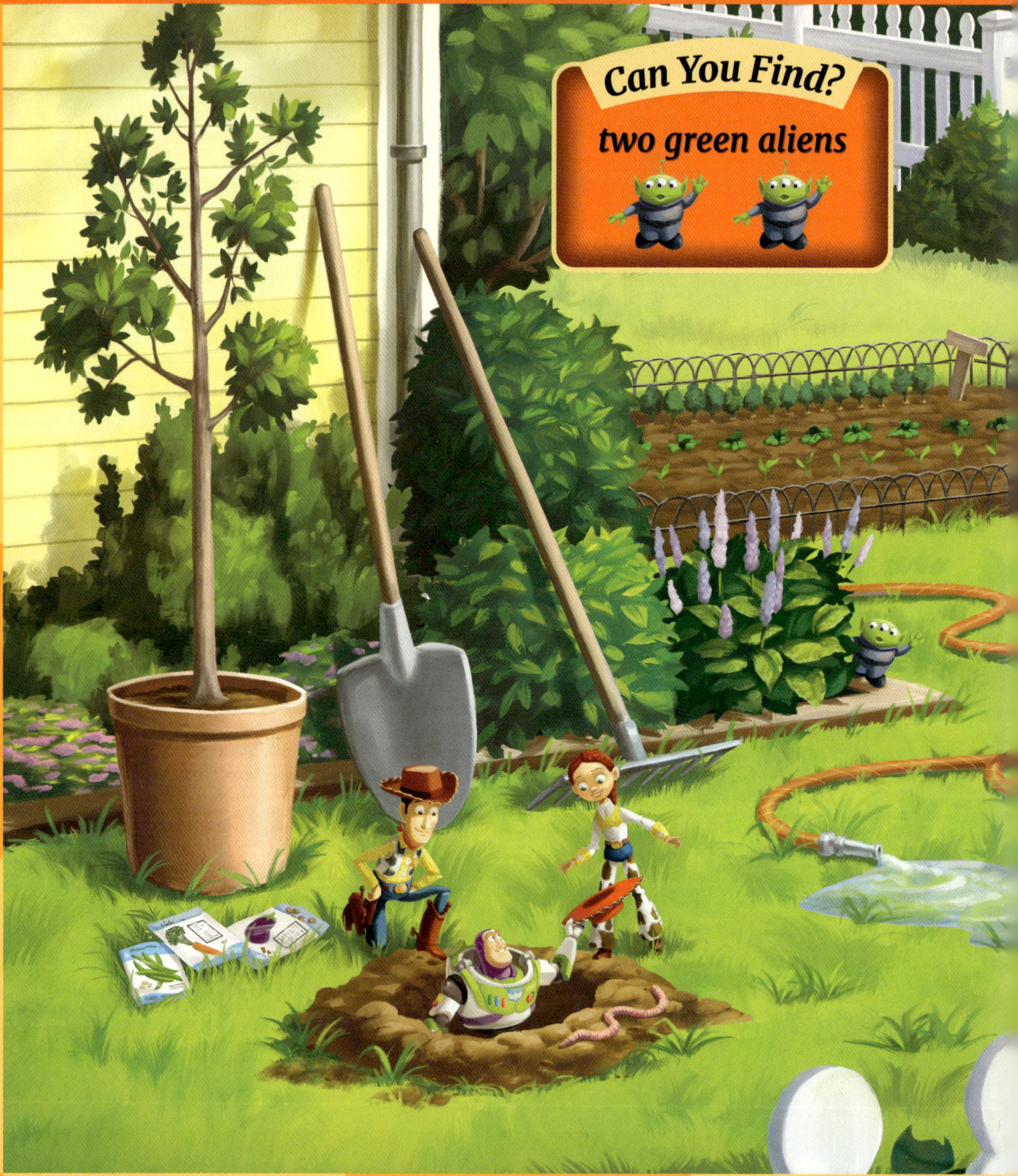
Can You Find?
two green aliens

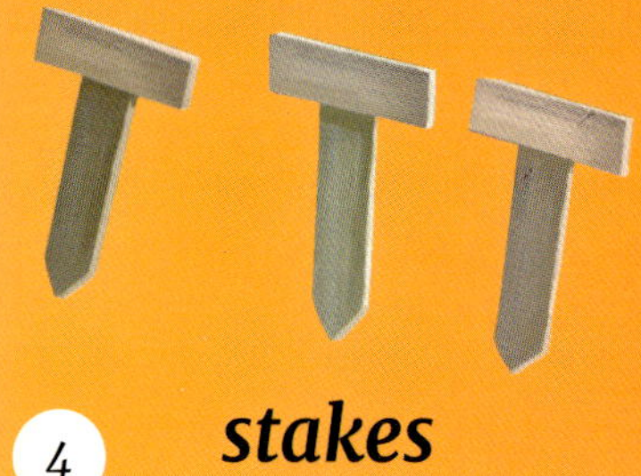

stakes

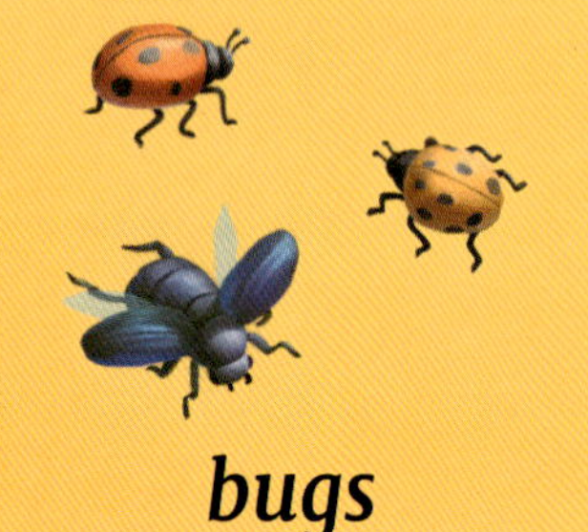

bugs

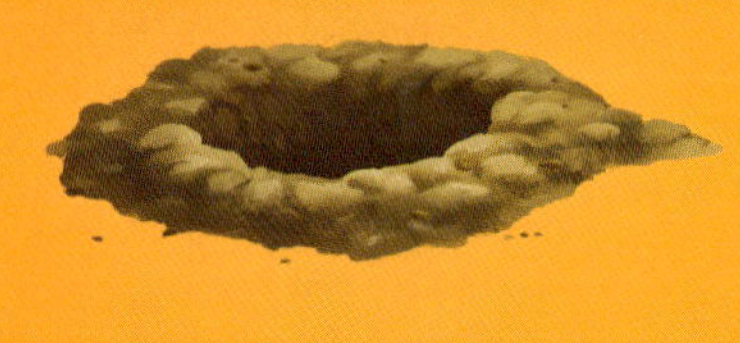

soil

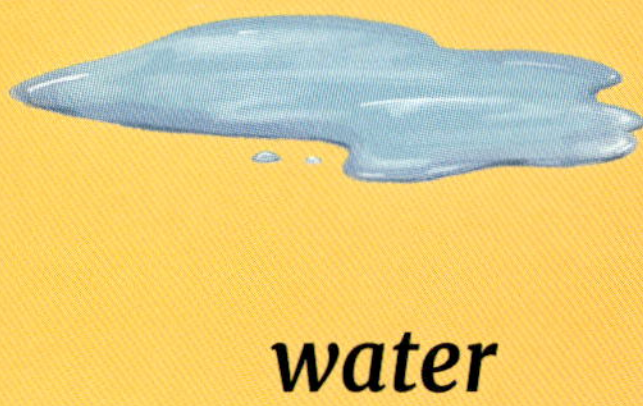

water

worm

bicycle

grass

hose

flowers

rake

tree

seeds

vegetable patch

snail

plants

# Mickey's House

stair

lawn mower

garden

porch

house

letter box

saw

toolbox

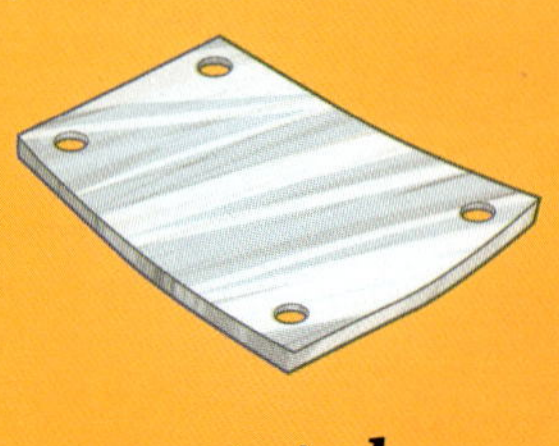
metal

wall

hammer

roof

letters

wood

door

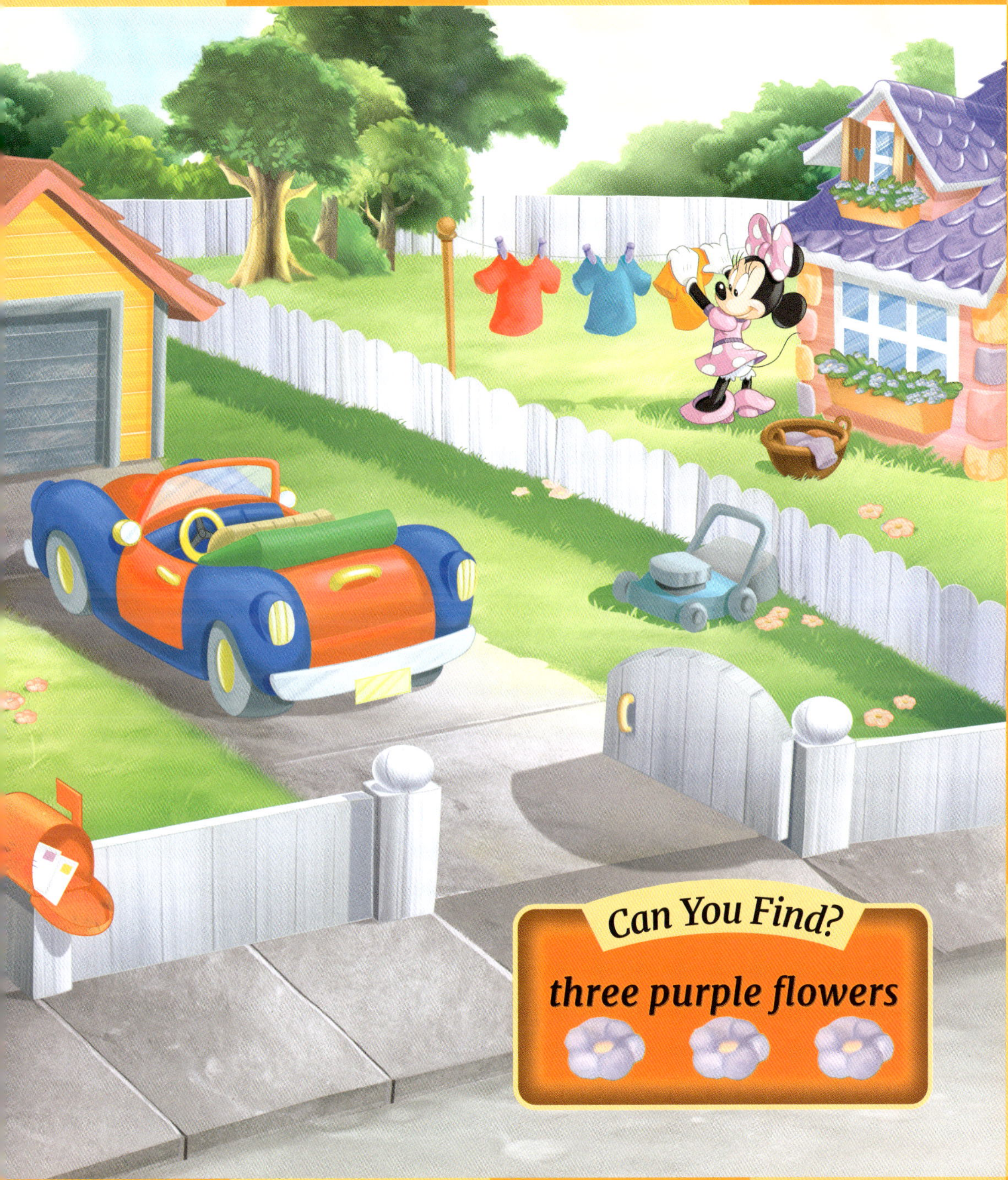

**Can You Find?**

*three purple flowers*

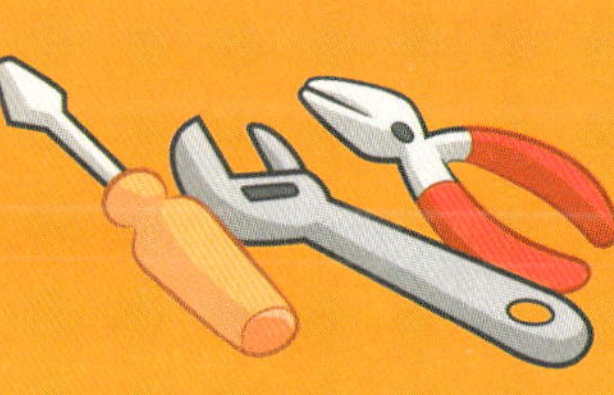
tools

nails

clothes

garage

car

# The Incredibles' Living Room

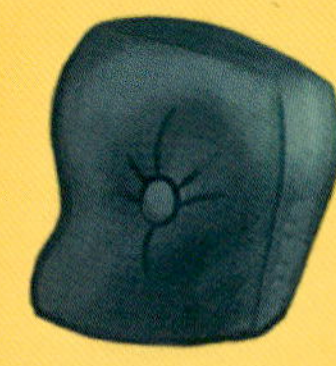
cushion

shelves

bookcase

television

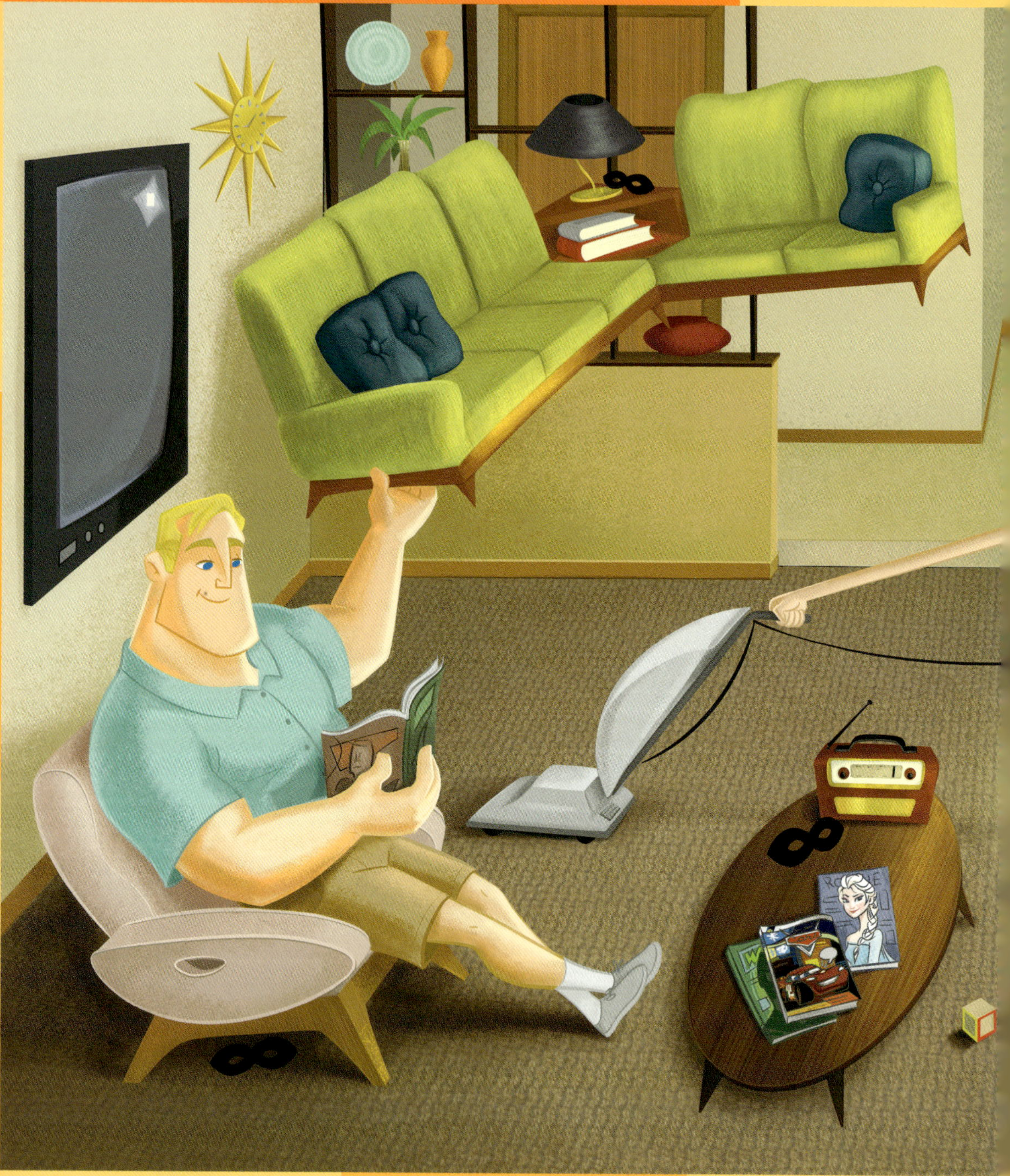

chair

vase

books

lamp

radio

clock

table

floor

vacuum cleaner

sofa

photos

**Can You Find?**

*five masks*

telephone

carpet

magazines

fireplace

# Belle and the Beast's Dining Room

*cloche*

*place mat*

*table*

*salt*

*dish*

*fork*

*cup*

*bowl*

spoon
jug
napkin
saucer
pepper
Can You Find?
a cupcake
candlestick
teapot
glass
sugar
knife
butter
cream

# Riley's Kitchen

rubber gloves

sink

mop

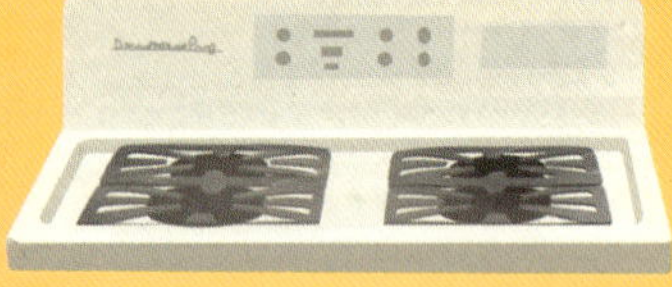
hob

bin

oven

iron

blender

pan

jar

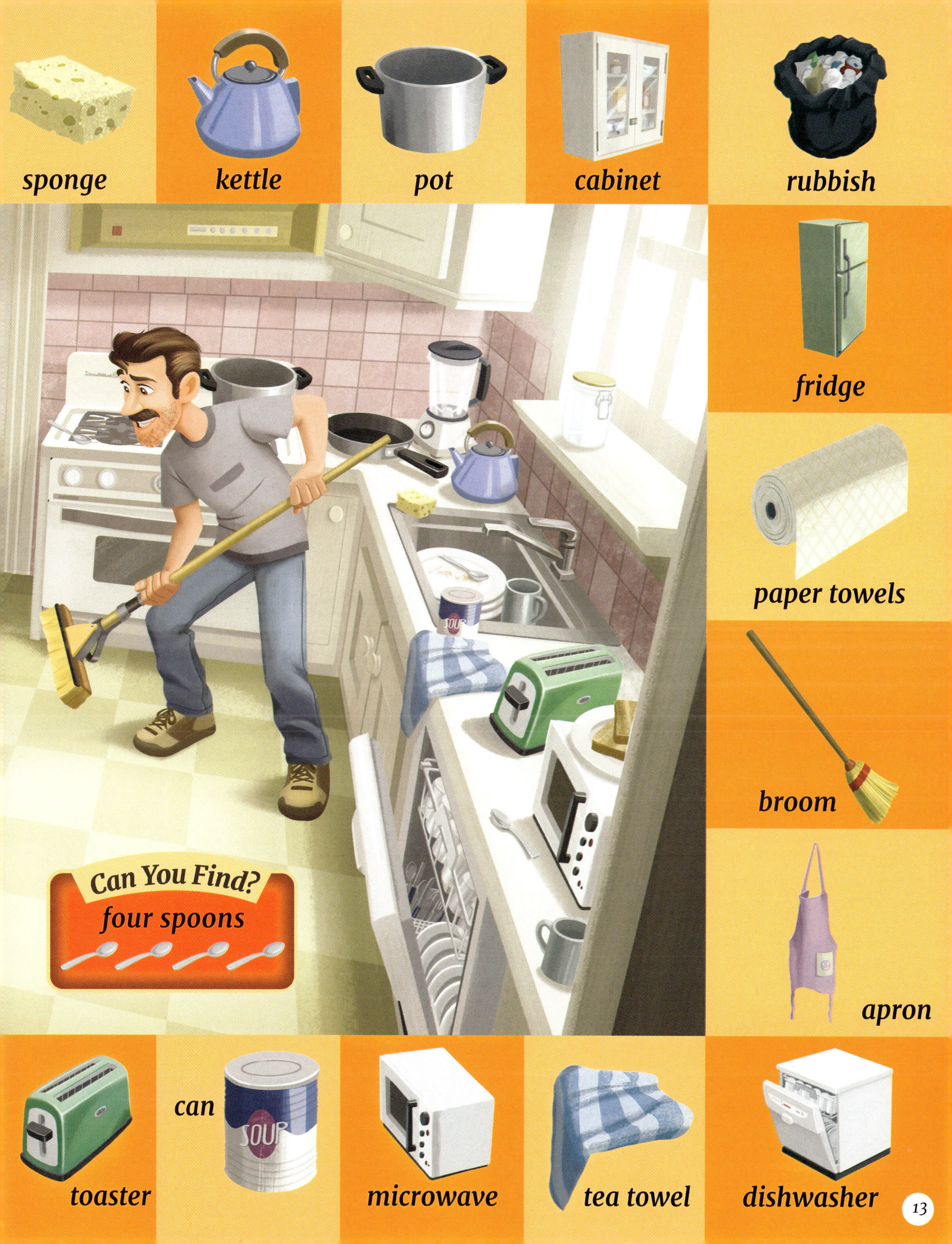

sponge

kettle

pot

cabinet

rubbish

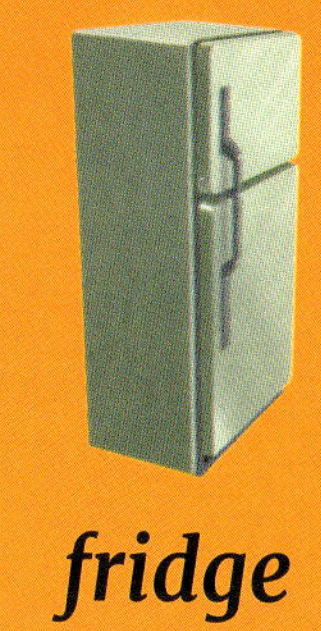
fridge

paper towels

broom

apron

**Can You Find?**
*four spoons*

toaster

can

microwave

tea towel

dishwasher

# Fine Meals with Remy

soup

eggs

roast beef

bacon

toast

ketchup

salad

jam

cereal

sausages

lobster

tea

steak

milk

burger

pasta

food
peanut butter
spaghetti
chicken
yoghurt
french fries
sandwich
fish
bread
rice
crackers
pizza
cheese
prawn
There's nothing like a good meal.
Is it time to eat yet?
meat
ham

# Delicious Produce with Tiana

onion

lettuce

beetroot

courgette

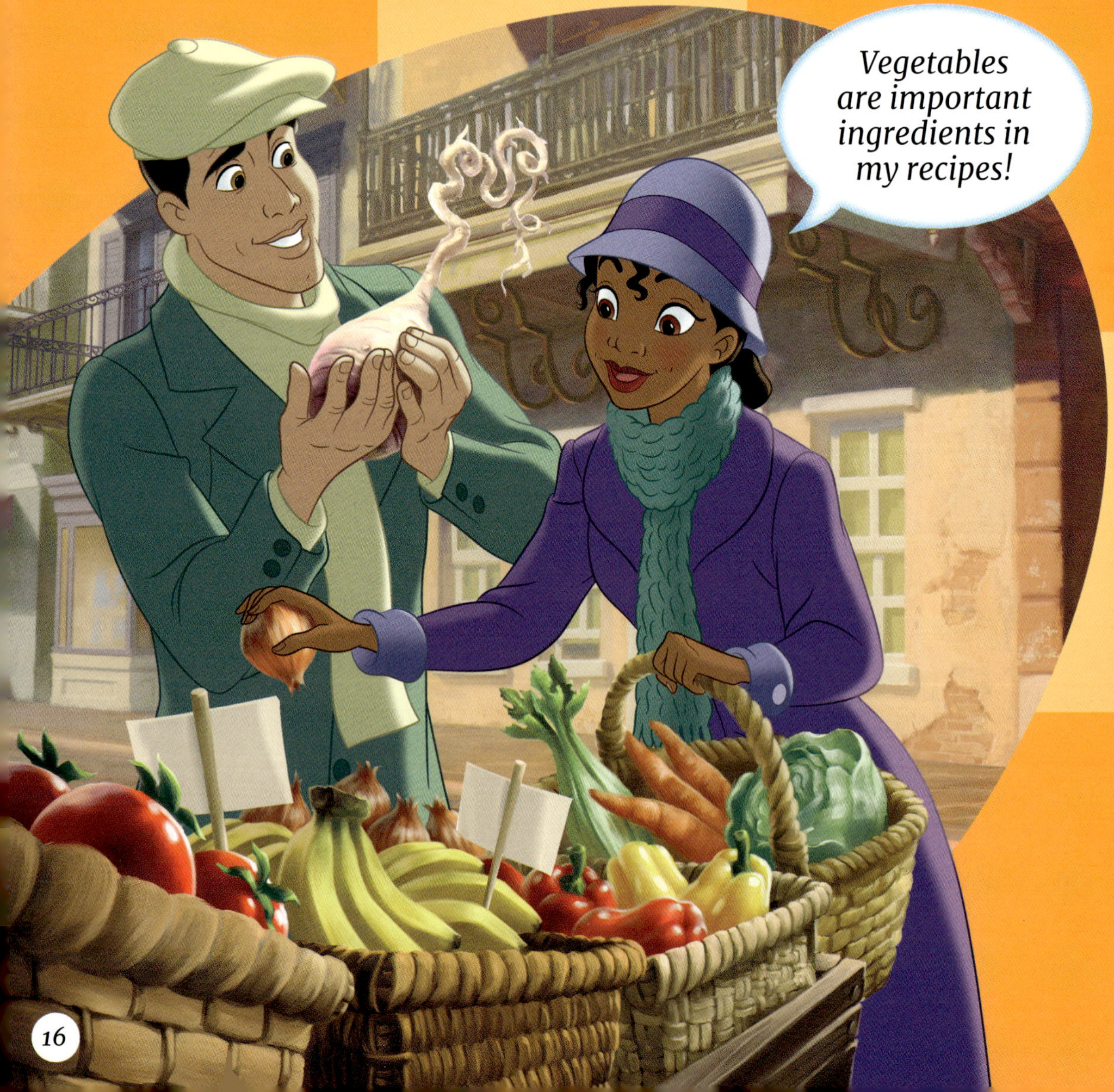

Vegetables are important ingredients in my recipes!

cauliflower

spinach

brussels sprouts

*mushrooms*

*potatoes*

*beans*

*garlic*

*aubergine*

*vegetables*

*cabbage*

*chillies*

*peas*

*green beans*

*peppers*

*olives*

*broccoli*

*pumpkin*

*tomato*

*corn*

*carrots*

*gherkins*

*celery*

*cucumber*

# Snow White's Feast of Fruits

pear

blackberries

melon

grapefruit

fig

raspberries

banana

papaya

coconut

blueberries

raisins

cherries

grapes

mango

orange

plum

fruit
peach
apple
strawberries
pineapple
avocado
lemon
watermelon
lime
I just love apples.
They're wonderful
in pies!

# Hiro's Bedroom

chest

poster

wardrobe

rug

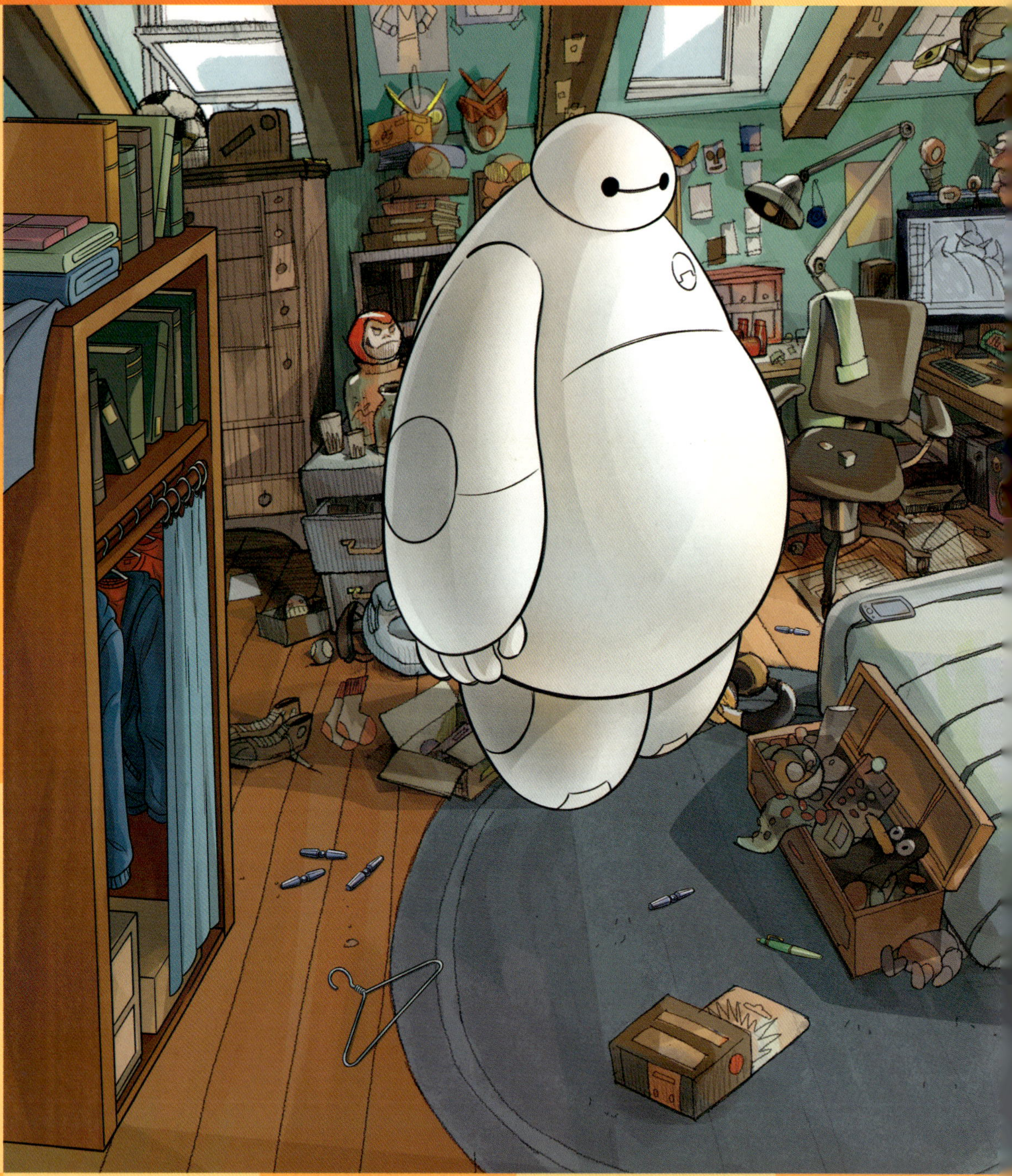

socks

phone

desk

drawer

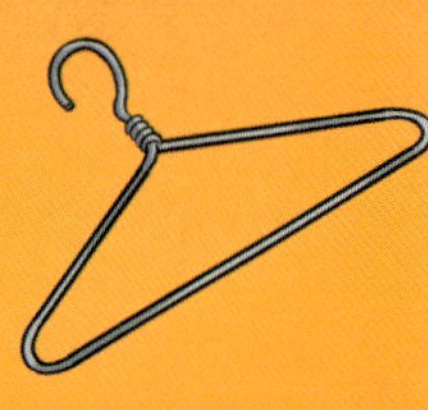
hanger

box
pillow
sheet
shelf
bed
fish tank
dresser
light
computer
picture
pencil
pen
shoes
paper
Can You Find?
five microbots

# What to Wear in Zootopia

umbrella

hat

skirt

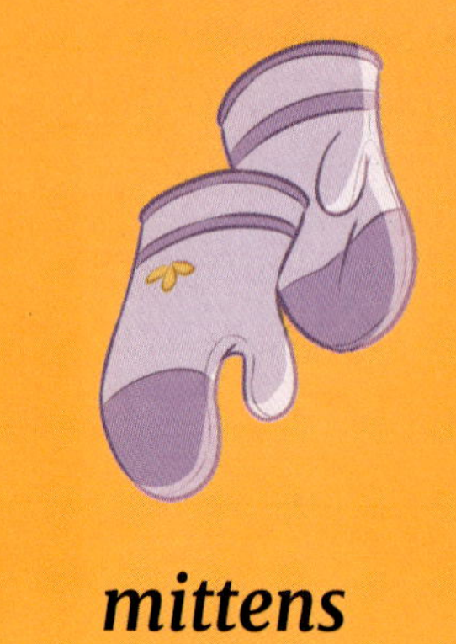

mittens

scarf

blouse

gown

jacket

button

tie

cap

shorts

bow

coat

jumper

T-shirt

suit
cape
trousers
gloves
belt
jeans
handbag
raincoat
shirt
dress
I love what you're wearing!
Looking sharp!

# In the Castle Nursery with Rapunzel

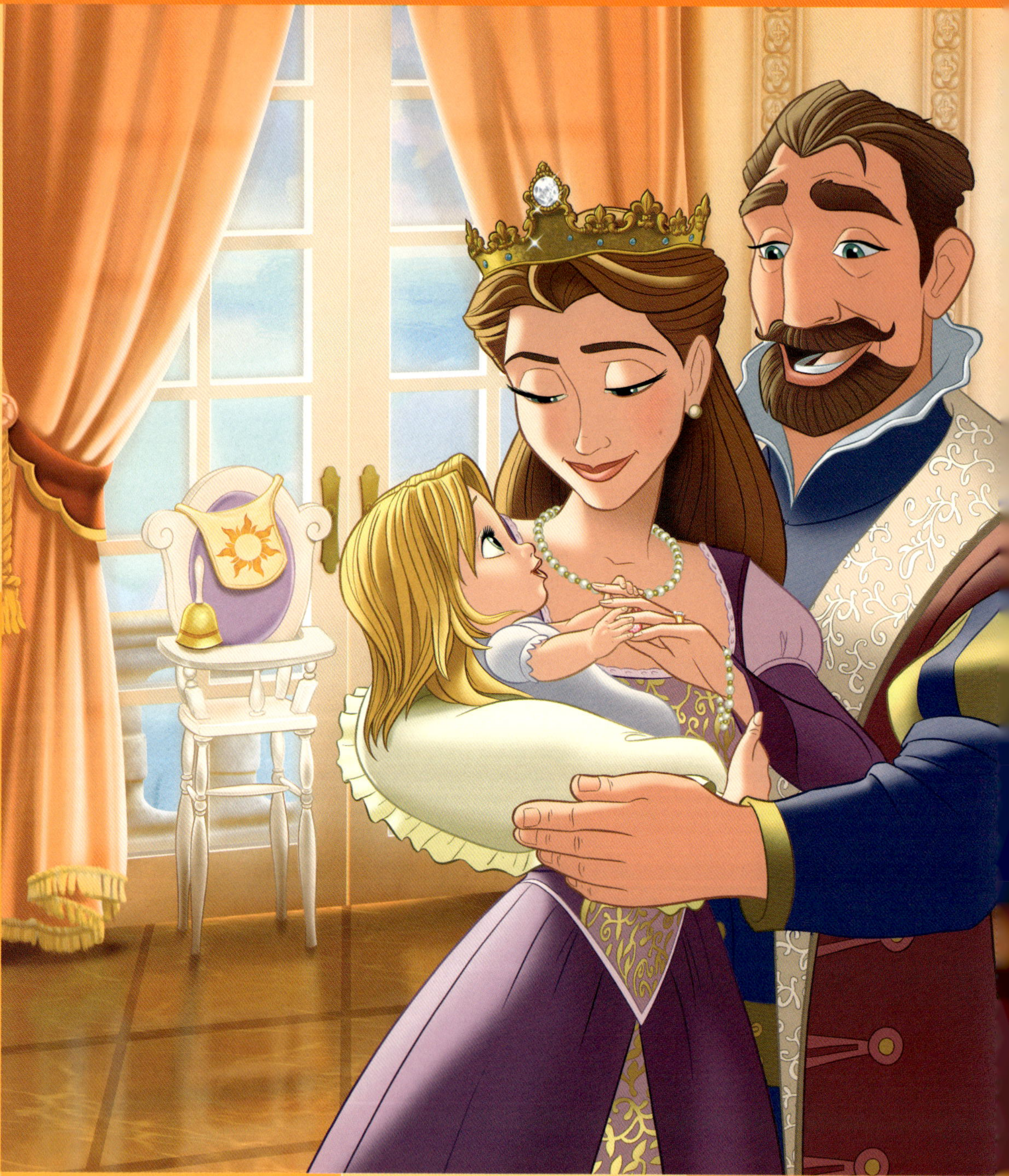

*mobile*

*high chair*

*key*

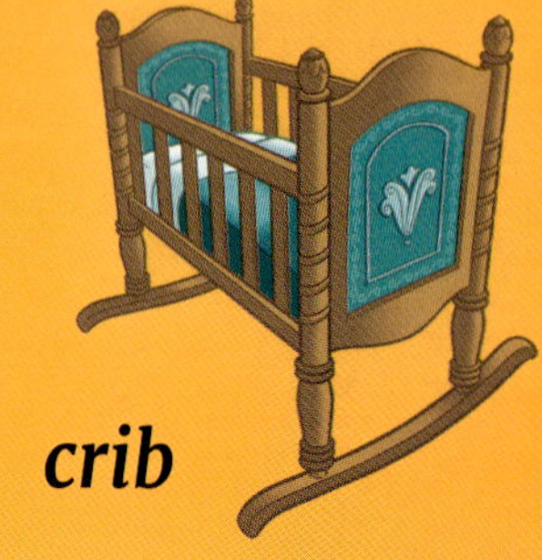

*crib*

*bell*

*ring*

crown

nappy

necklace

## Can You Find?

four suns

bottle

teddy bear

rattle

bib

blanket

baby

# Donald's Bathroom

bath mat

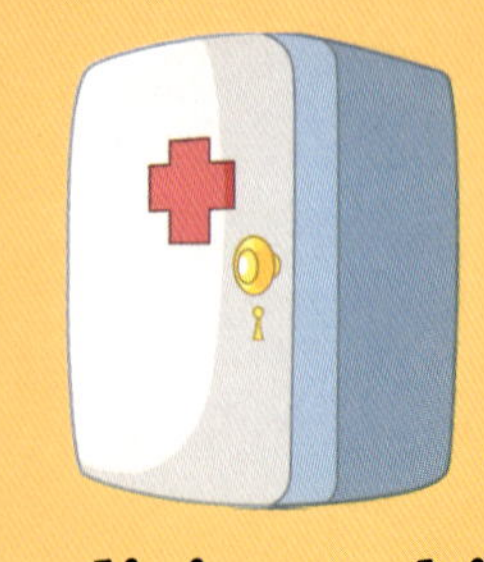

medicine cabinet

toy boat

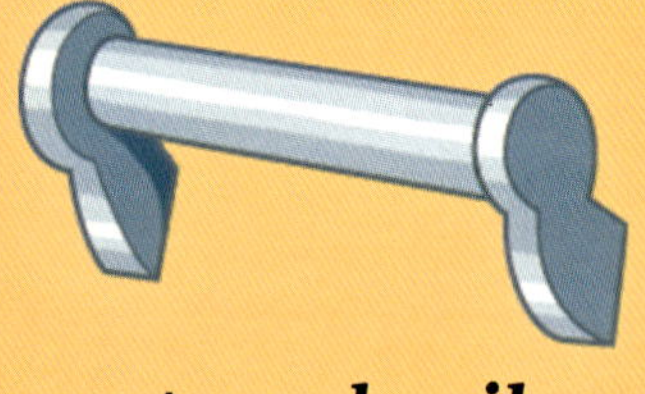

towel rail

wallpaper

toothpaste

comb

soap

flannel

toilet paper

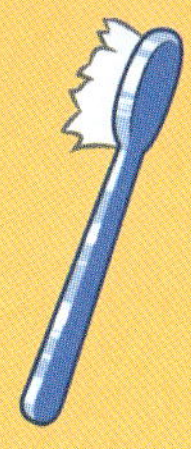

toothbrush

bath towel

robe

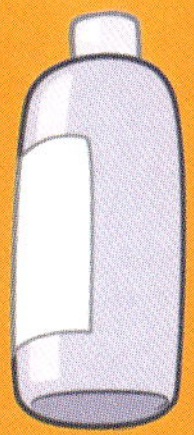

shampoo

shower

bubbles

toilet

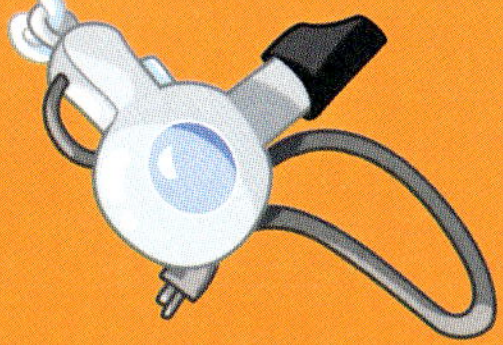

hair dryer

**Can You Find?**

three rubber ducks

brush

shower cap

mirror

bath

# Hiro and Baymax Explore the City

*bus stop*

*office building*

*bus*

*billboard*

*restaurant*

*people*

*stop sign*

newspaper

florist

grocery shop

bank

library

tram

cinema

**Can You Find?**

four lanterns

buildings

city

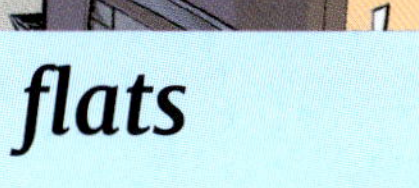

flats

street

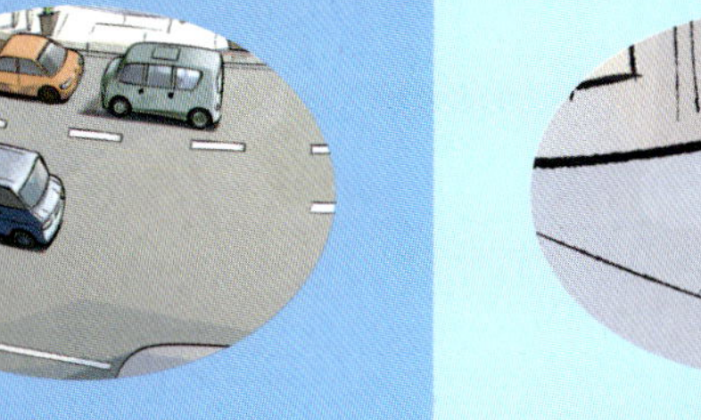

traffic light

# In the Village with Rapunzel and Flynn

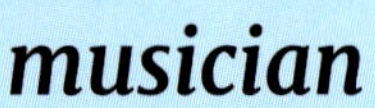

*musician*

*dancers*

*sign*

*awning*

*bucket*

*flowers*

boy

village

roof

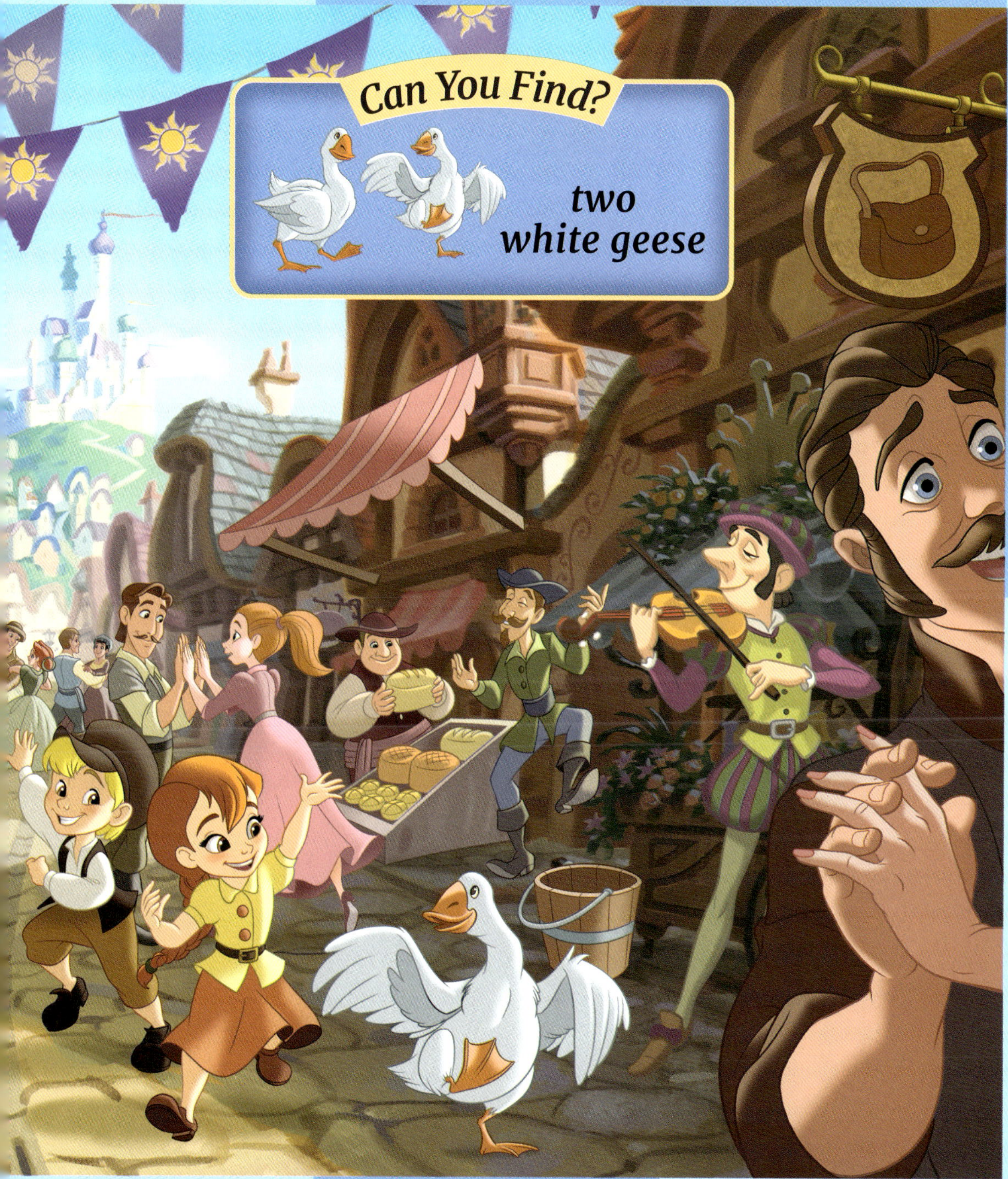

## Can You Find?

two white geese

bakery

castle

wagon

bag

chimney

girl

# Mike and Sulley at School

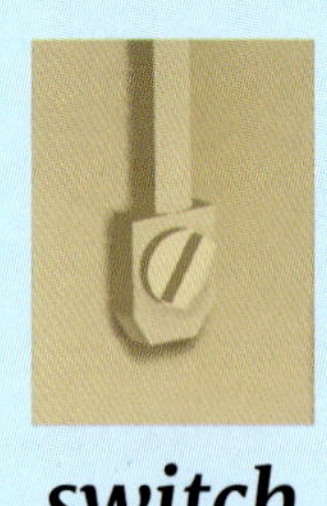

switch

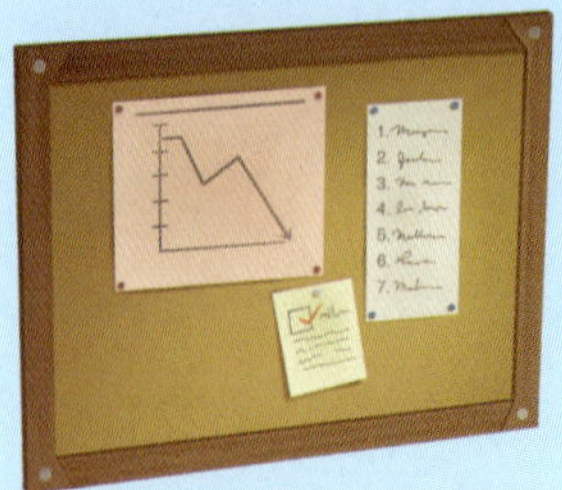

bulletin board

notebook

blackboard

scissors

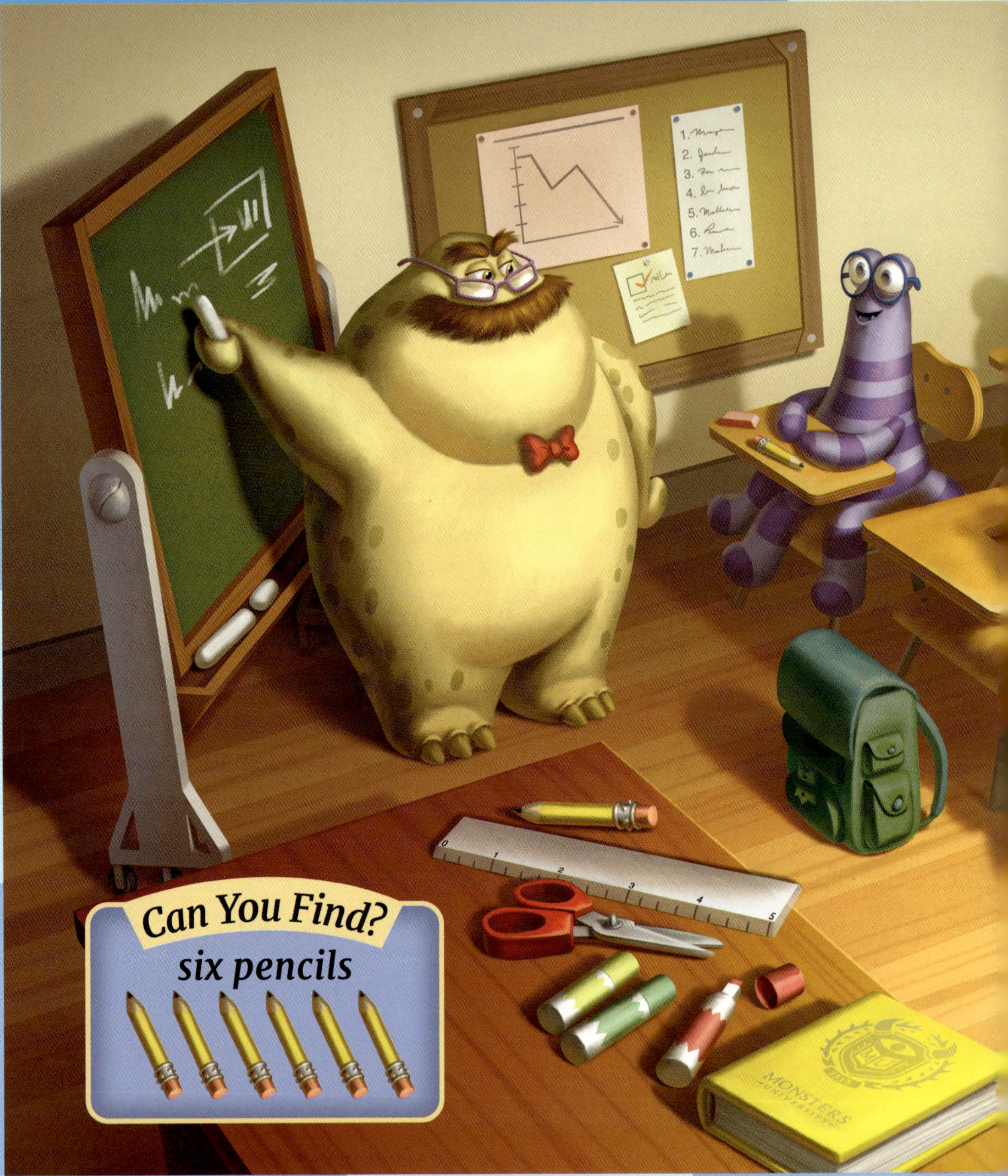

**Can You Find?**

six pencils

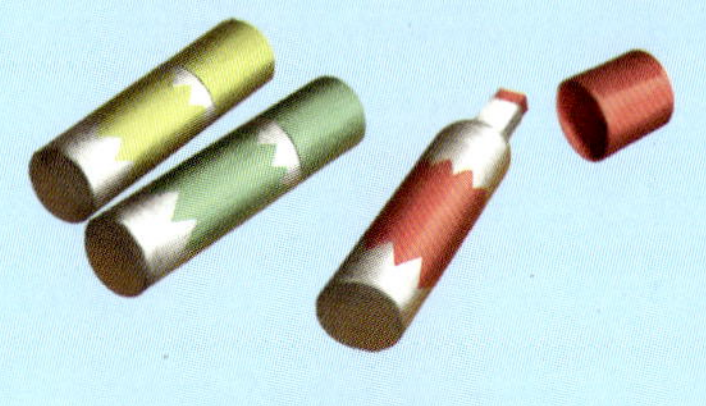

markers

tick

textbook

eraser

*picture*

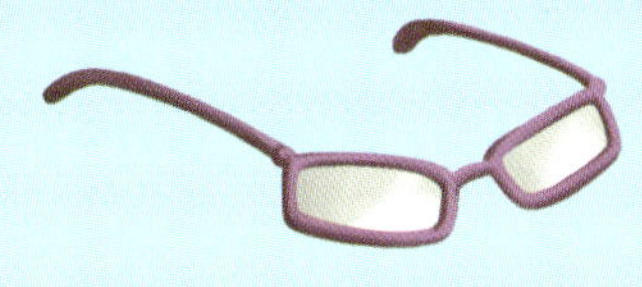

*glasses*

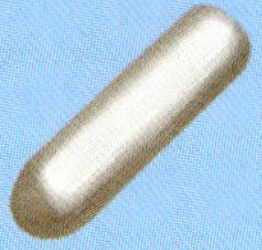

*chalk*

*teacher*

*ruler*

*class*

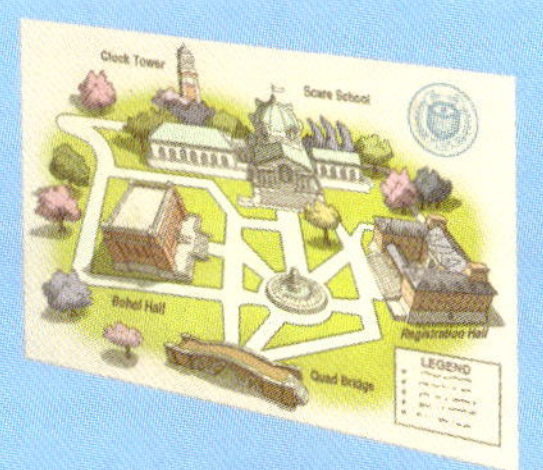

*map*

*student*

*list*

*flag*

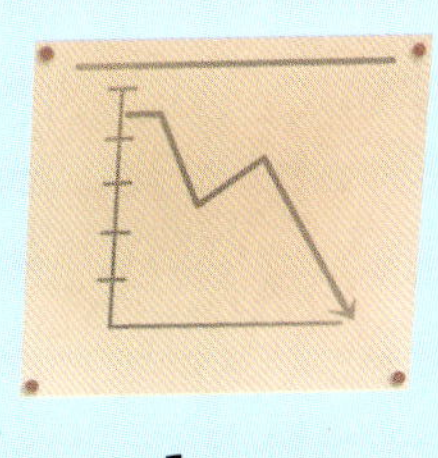

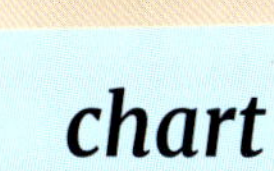

*chart*

*backpack*

# At Tiana's Restaurant

chandelier

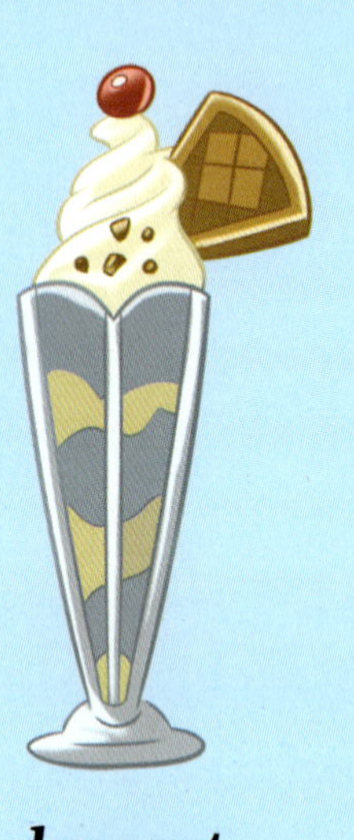
dessert

waiter

coins

wallet

receipt

tray

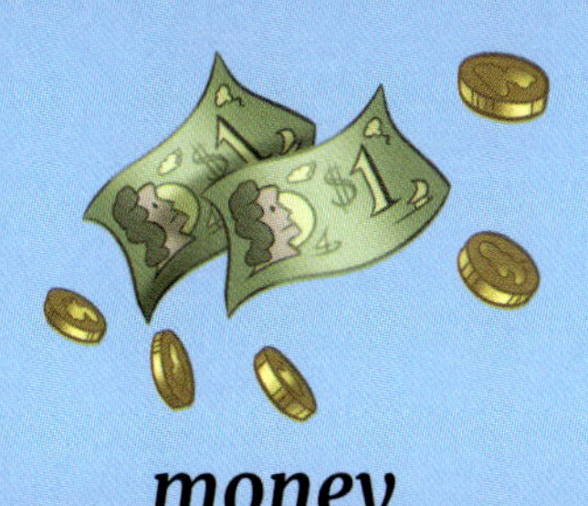

money

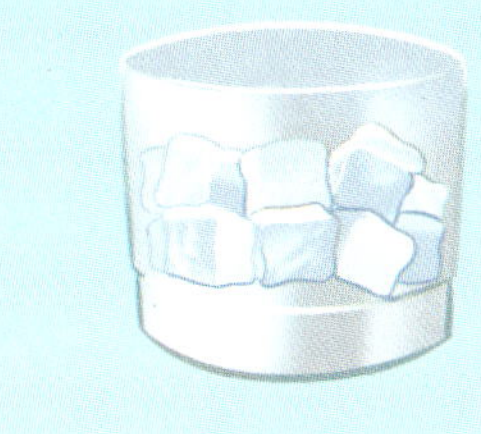

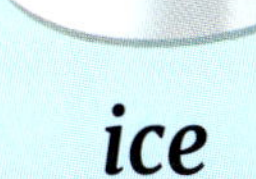

ice

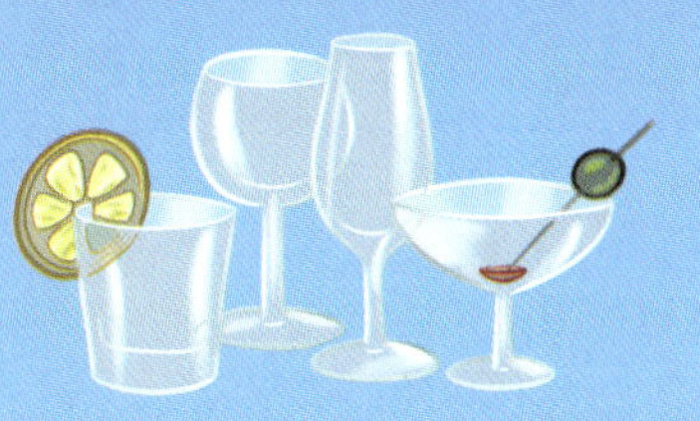

drinks

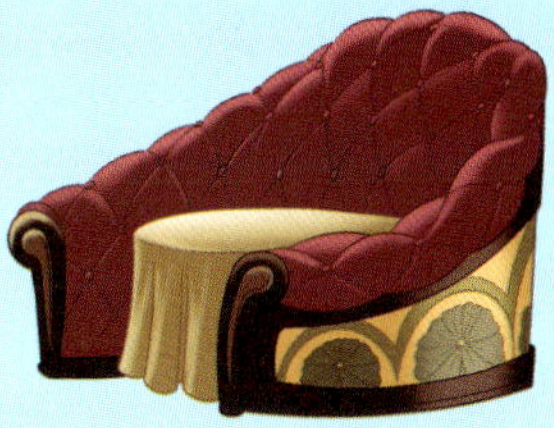

booth

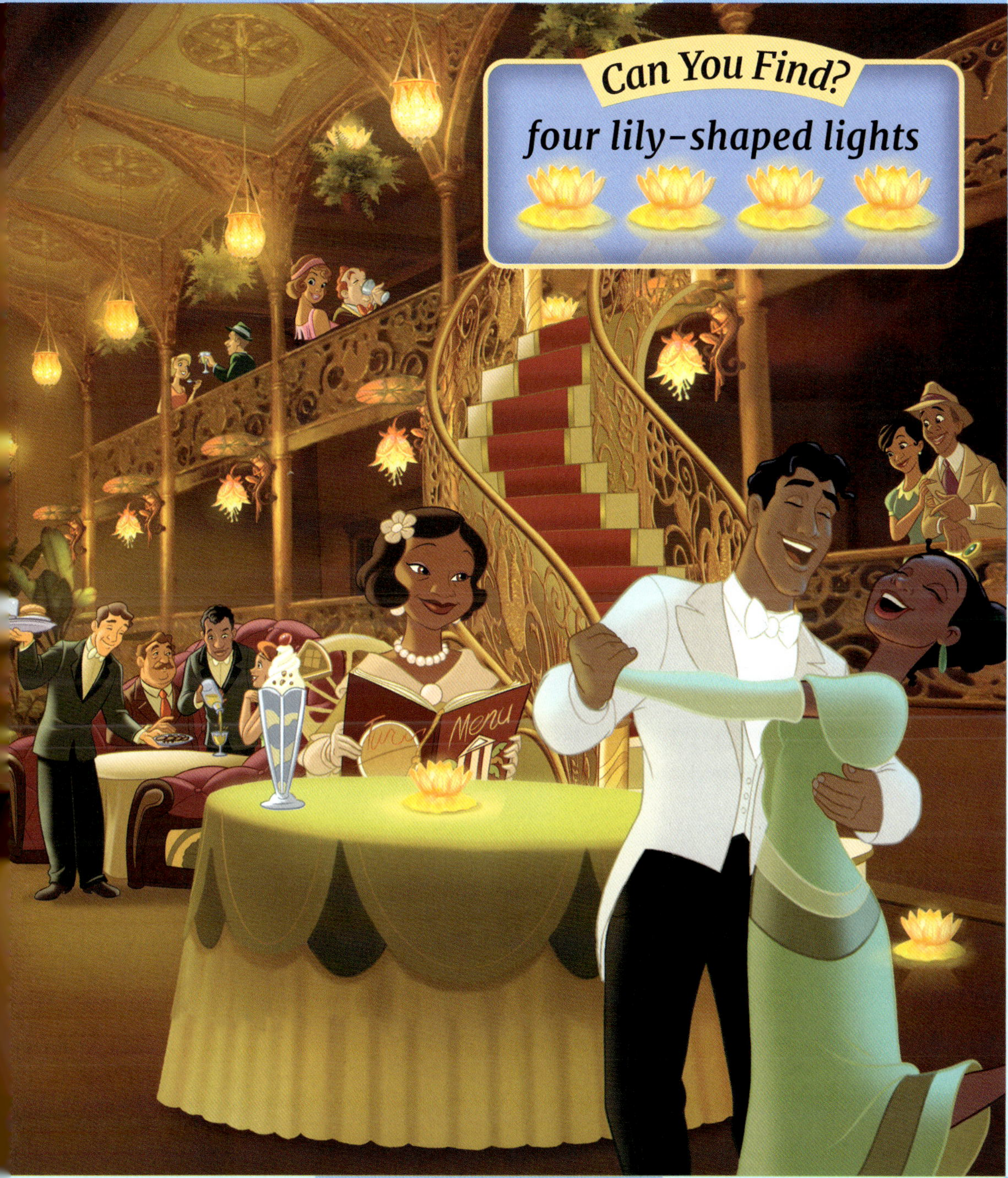

Can You Find?
four lily-shaped lights
Menu

waitress

stairs

bottle

plate

Menu
menu

$1
banknote

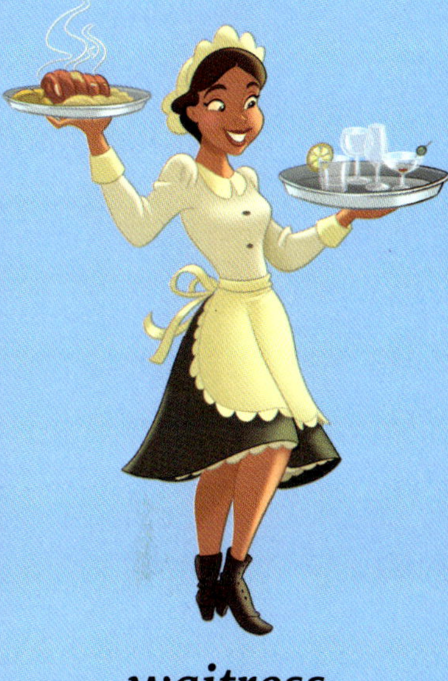

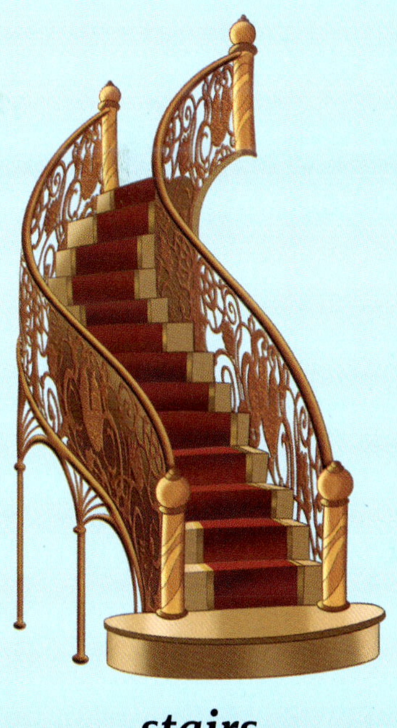

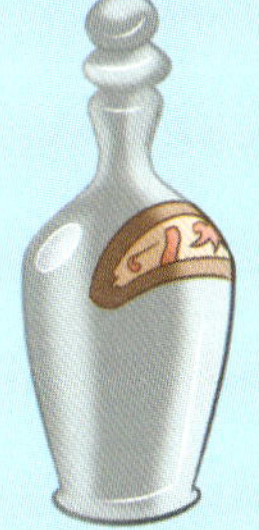

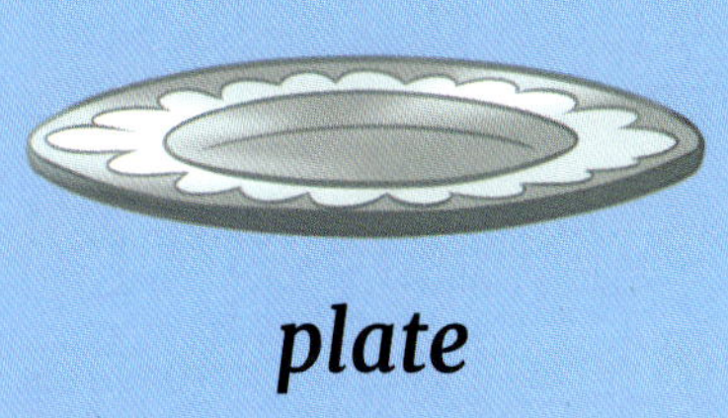

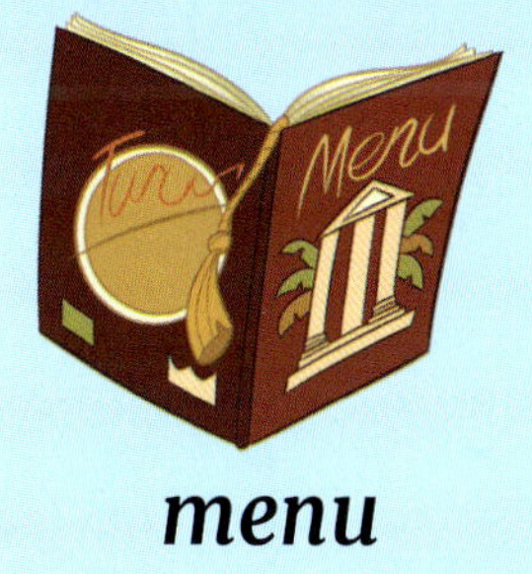

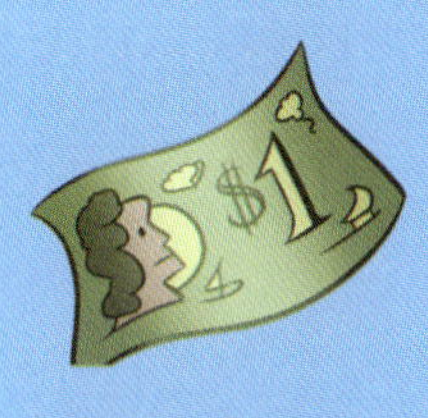

# Minnie and Friends Go Shopping

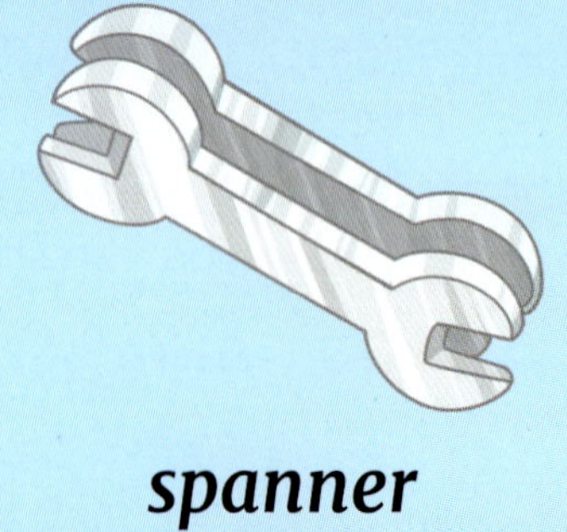

spanner

screwdrivers

silver

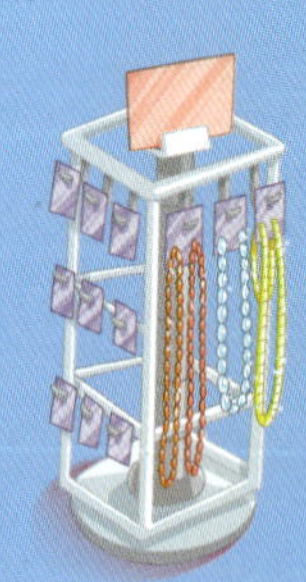

necklaces

tablet

watch

laptop

pliers

mobile phone

gold

headphones

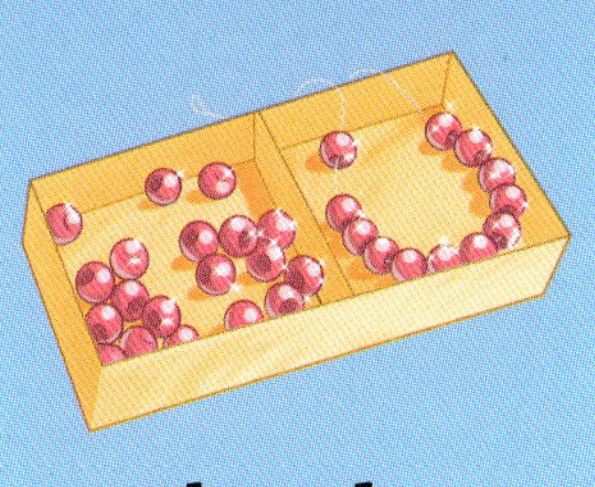

beads

calculator

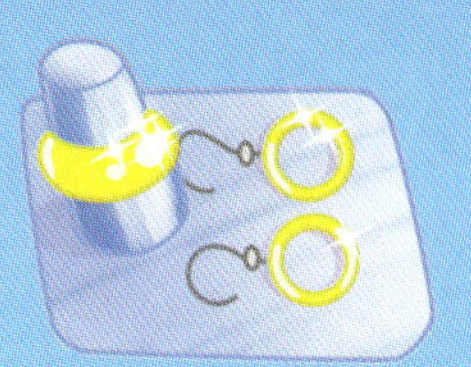

jewellery

music player

angle grinder

earrings

camera

bracelets

**Can You Find?**

two diamonds

drill

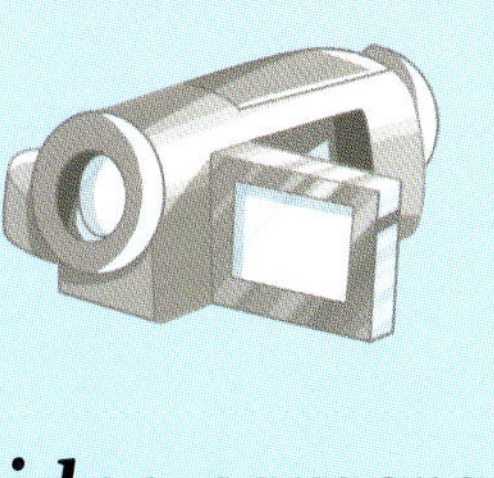

video camera

printer

hacksaw

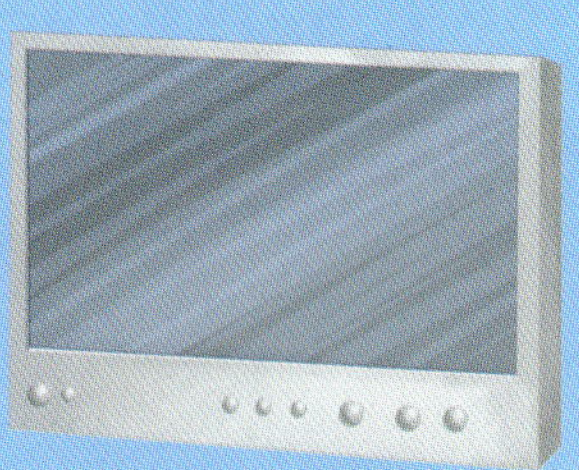

TV

# Buzz Lightyear in the Toy Shop

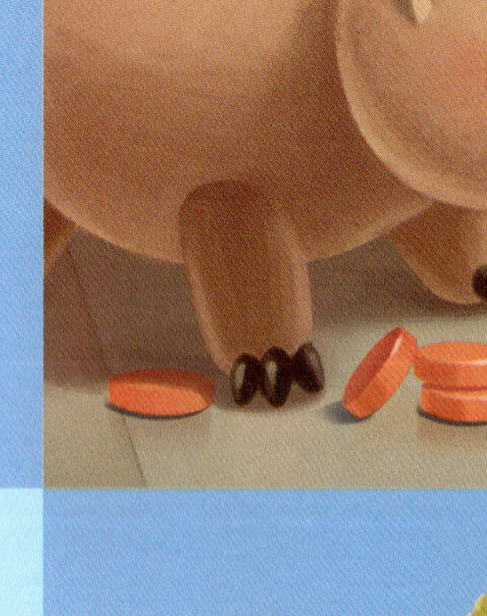

stuffed animals

toy soldier

puzzle

doll

dinosaur

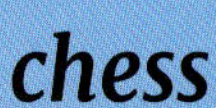

chess

video game

draughts

board game

action figure

yo-yo

ball

**Can You Find?**

seven green army men

spinning top

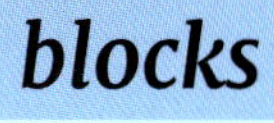

blocks

toy car

toys

playing cards

piggy bank

rocket

# Lilo and Stitch at the Market

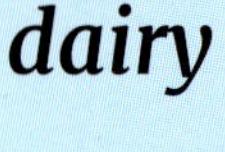

dairy

till

cashier

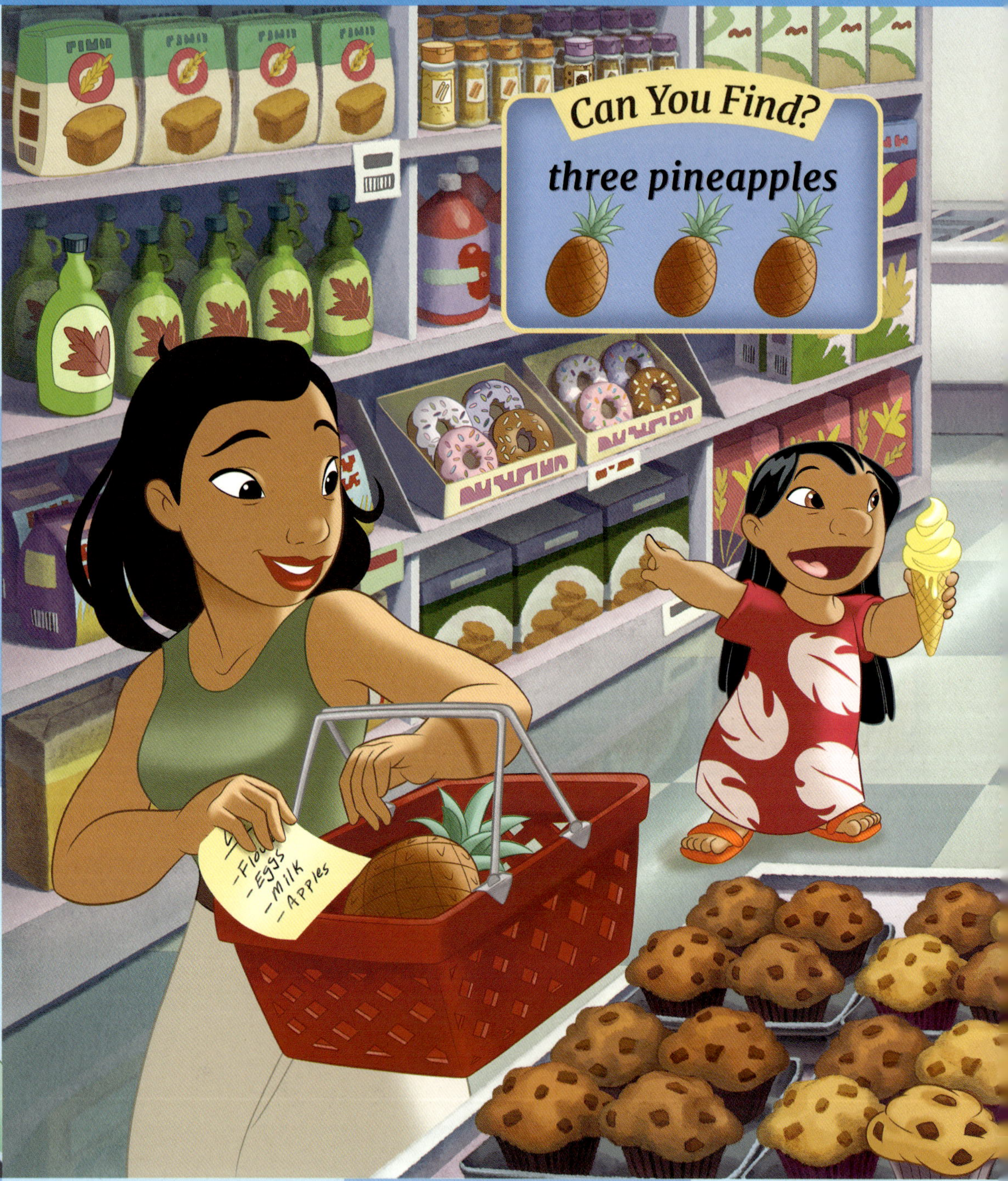

Can You Find?

three pineapples

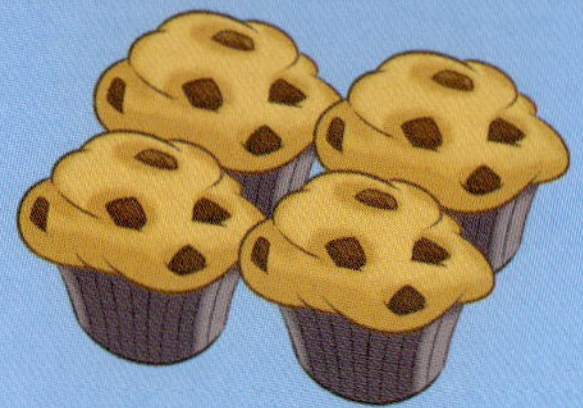

muffins

credit card

doughnuts

flour

*basket*

*shopping bag*

*syrup*

*seafood*

*shopping list*

*fruit juice*

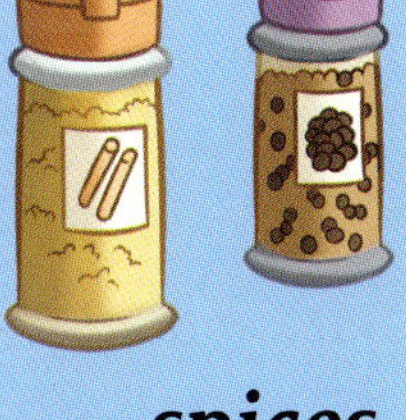

*spices*

*ice cream*

*waffles*

*trolley*

# Goofy Visits the Doctor's Office

mask

nurse

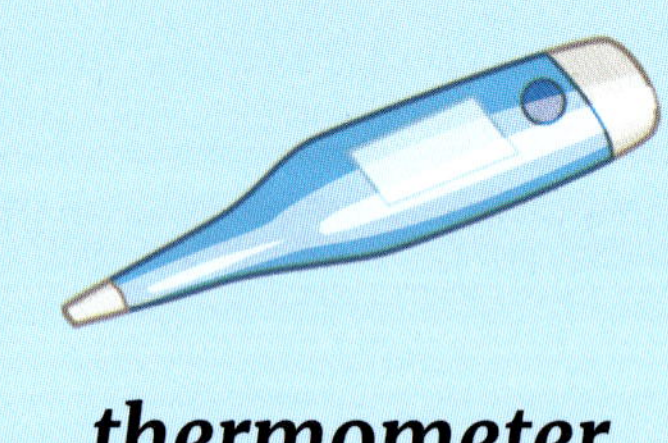

thermometer

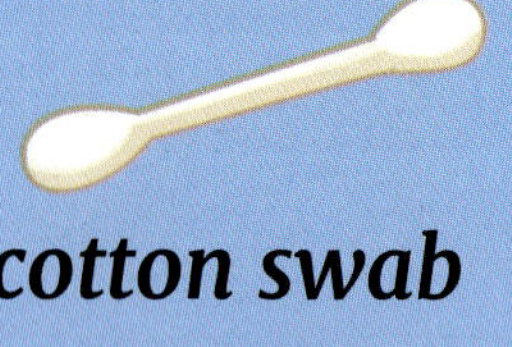

cotton swab

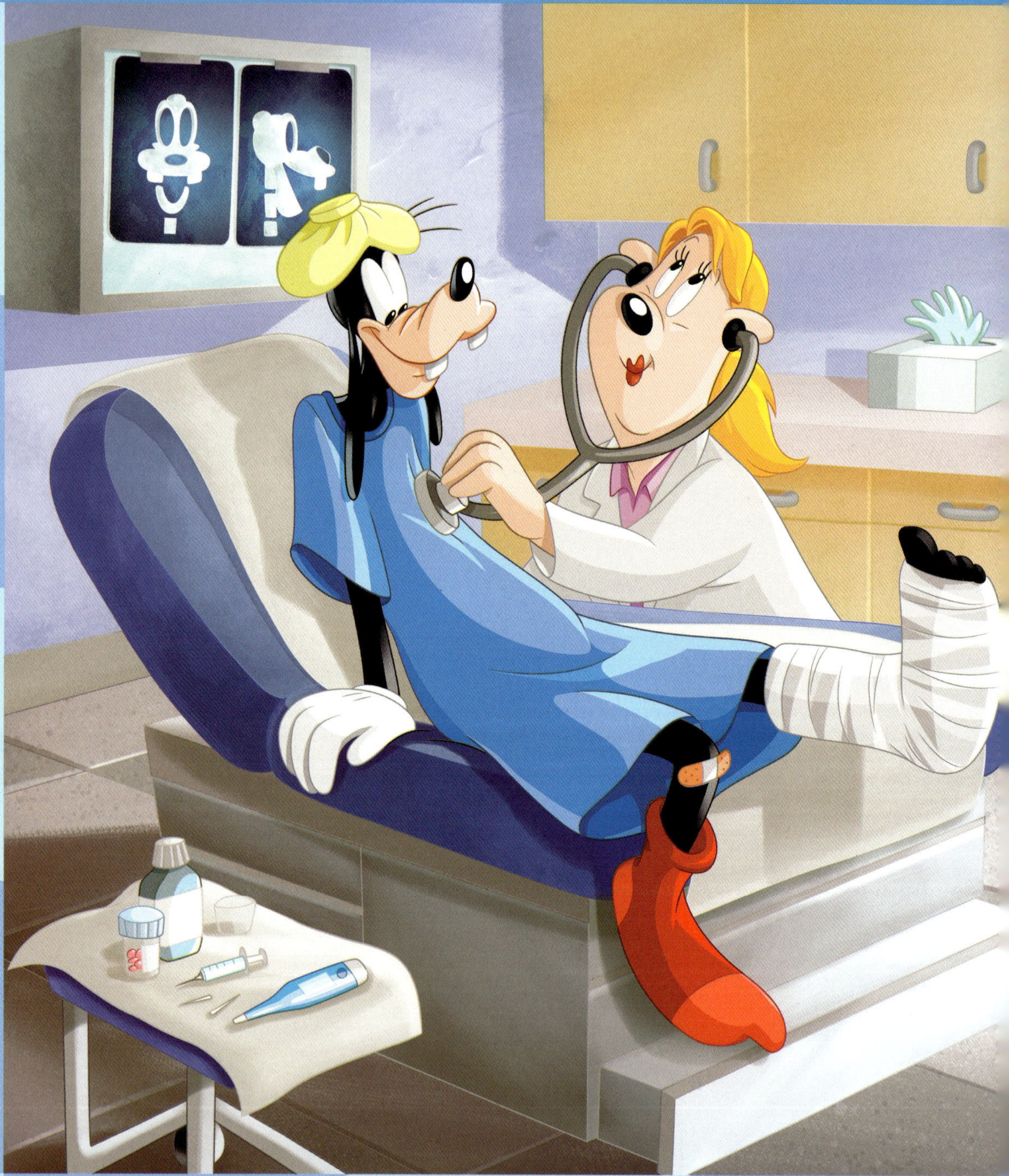

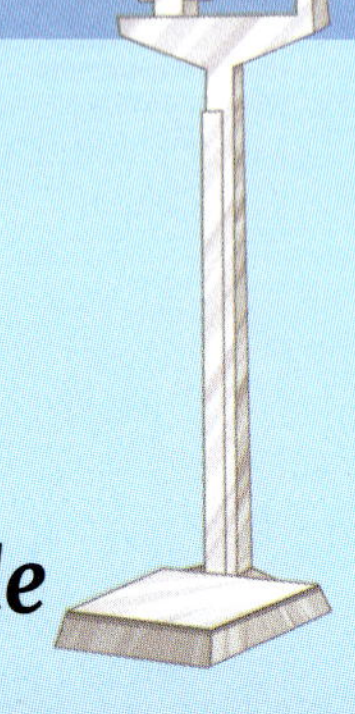

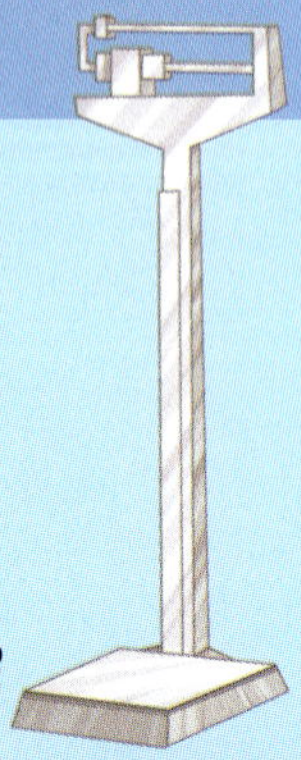

scale

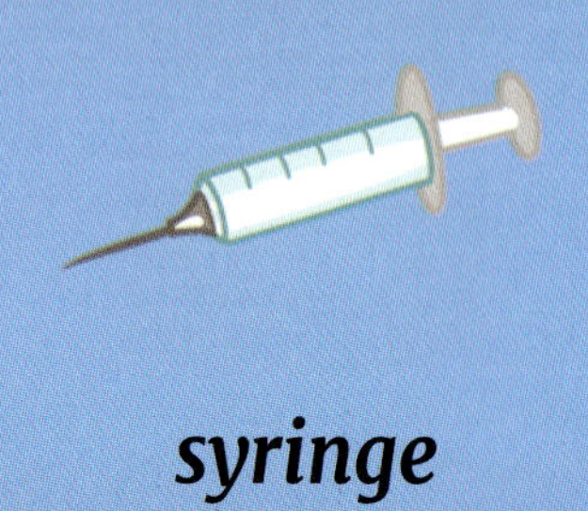

syringe

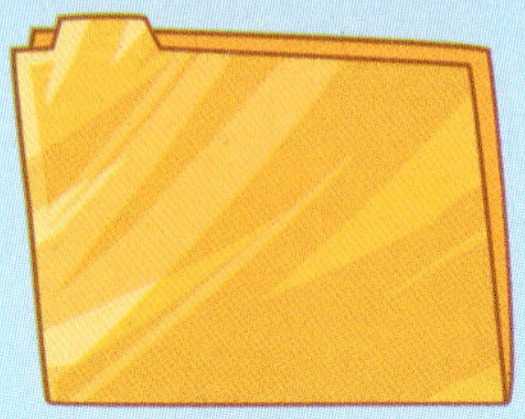

file

cotton wool

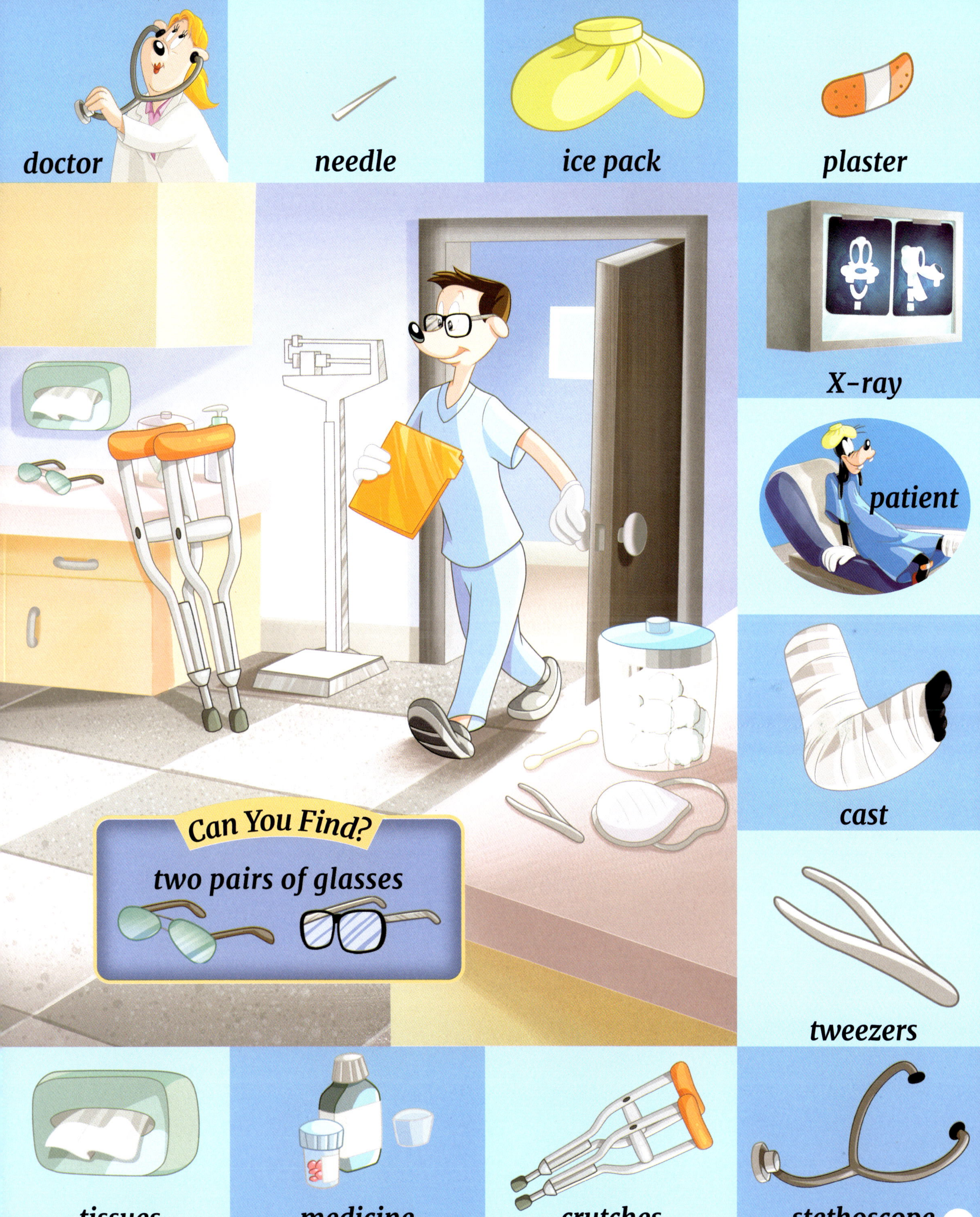
doctor
needle
ice pack
plaster
X-ray
patient
cast
tweezers
Can You Find?
two pairs of glasses
tissues
medicine
crutches
stethoscope

# Mammals at Work in Zootopia

plumber

engineer

nurse

dancer

athlete

dentist

banker

mechanic

construction worker

reporter

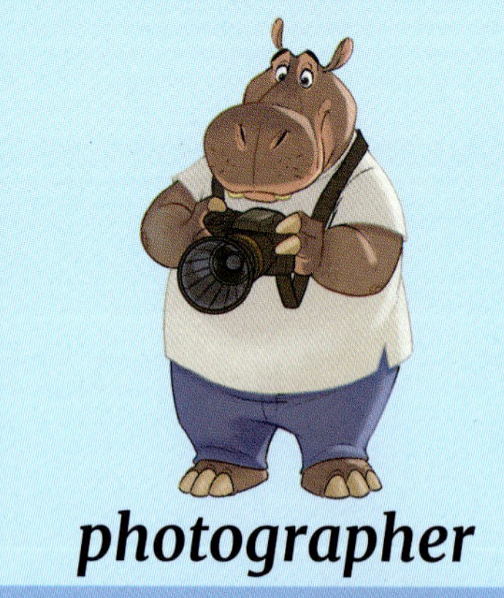
photographer

driver

police officer

chef

carpenter

farmers

clerk
singer
astronaut
doctor
secretary
firefighter
librarian
magician
painter
In Zootopia, anyone can be anything!

# Lightning Goes for a Drive

*pick-up truck*

*boat*

*snowplough*

*bulldozer*

*ship*

*How about going for a drive?*

*Great idea!*

motorcycle

van

submarine

lorry

plough

ambulance

rubbish truck

car

rocket ship

tractor

crane

jet

school bus

tow truck

tank

ferry

train

plane

bus

taxi

# Mickey and Friends at the Airport

passenger

captain

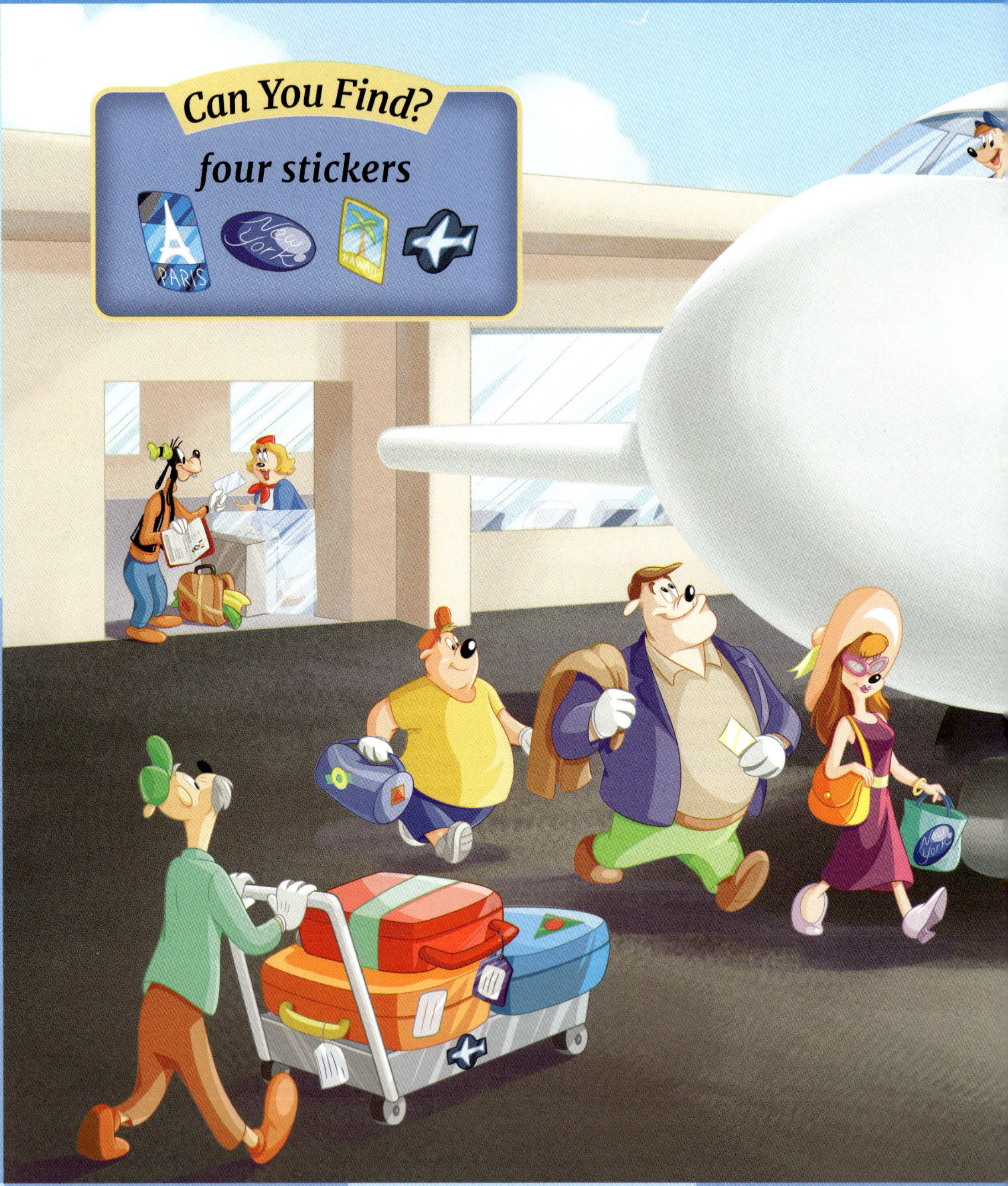

Can You Find?

four stickers

PARIS

New York

HAWAII

wing

sky

line

passport

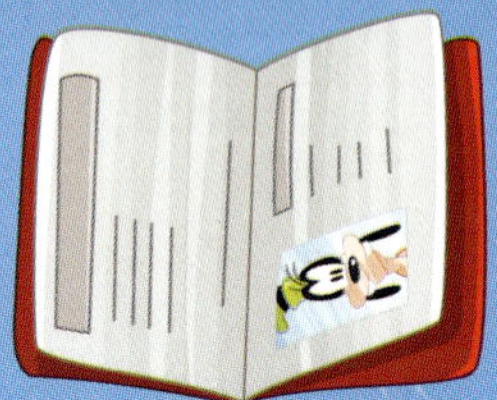

*aeroplane*

*luggage*

*propeller*

*helicopter*

*pilot*

*flight attendant*

*tag*

*engine*

*ground*

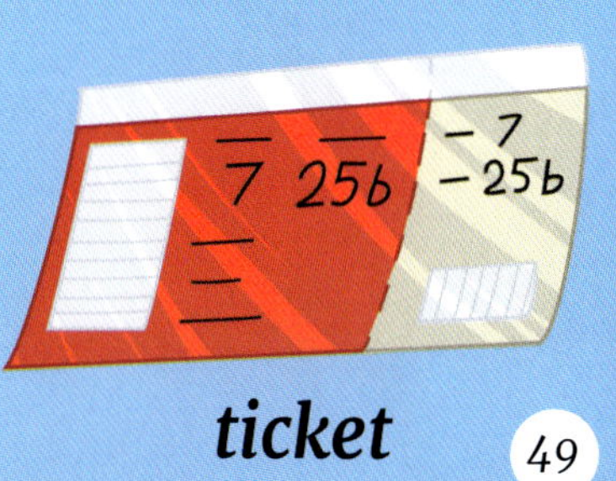
*ticket*

# The Incredibles Protect the City

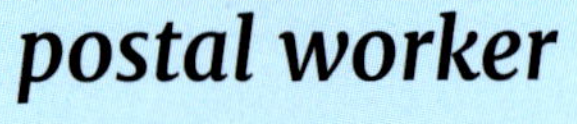

*postal worker*

*Supers*

*police officer*

*axe*

*postcards*

*package*

*helmet*

fire

alarm

badge

firefighter

post office

ladder

heroes

POST OFFICE

**Can You Find?**

three arrows

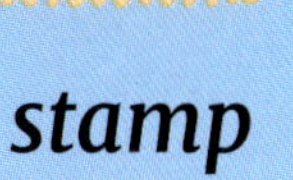

stamp

mail

fire hydrant

wheel

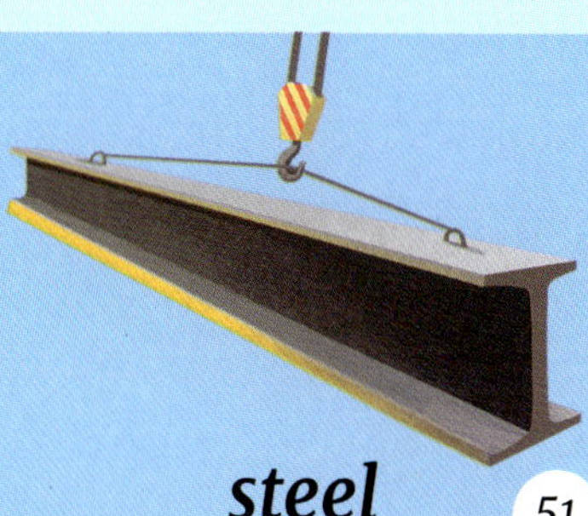

steel

# Mickey and Minnie Plan a Day of Fun

team

fireworks

board

play

theatre

rollercoaster

zoo

amusement park

parade

hike

camp

circus

cage

museum

# A Picnic in Zootopia

fountain

flag

Can You Find?

four doughnuts

rubbish bin

lake

picnic

friends

wind
bench
park
statue
kite
runner
picnic blanket
string
path

# Buzz and Woody at the Playground

seesaw

skates

crayons

**Can You Find?**

*five stars*

☆ ☆ ☆ ☆ ☆

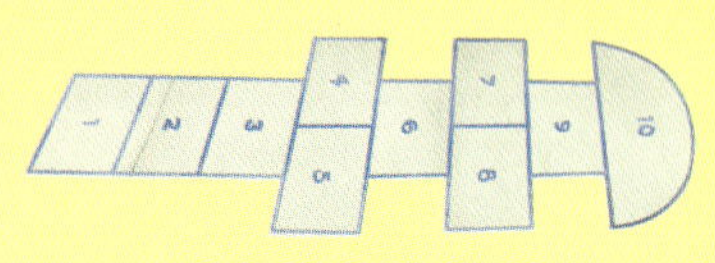

hopscotch

spade

bucket

sandpit

skateboard

handle

climbing frame

marbles

tricycle

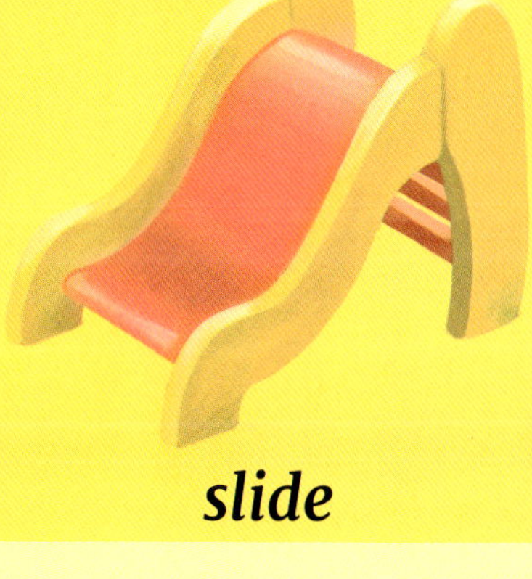
slide

play area

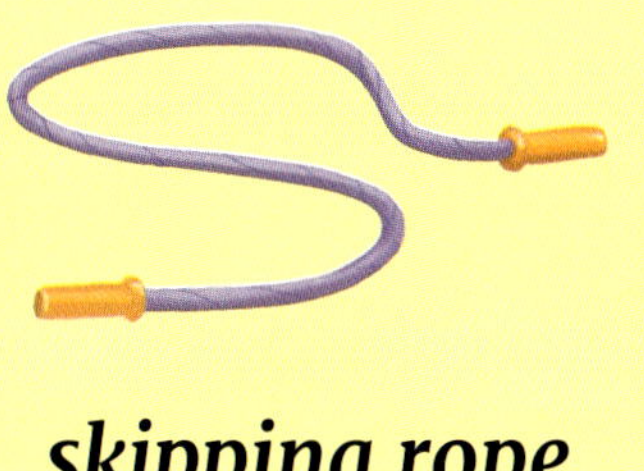
skipping rope

tag

swing

bar

HAVING
FUN

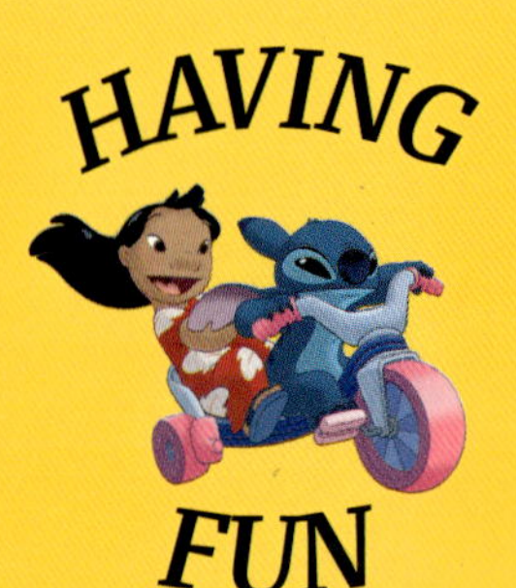

# Lilo and Stitch at the Science Museum

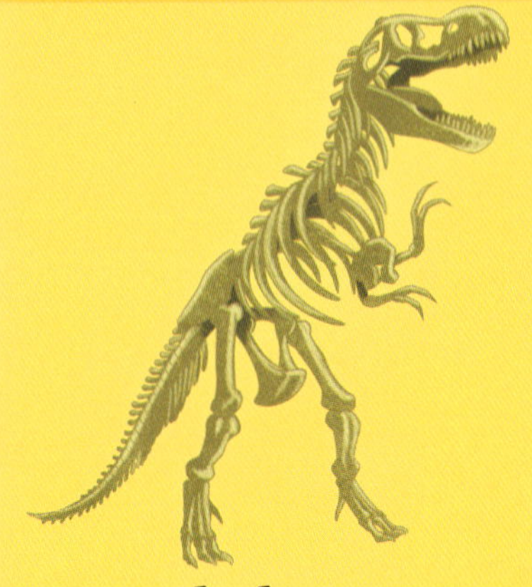

*skeleton*

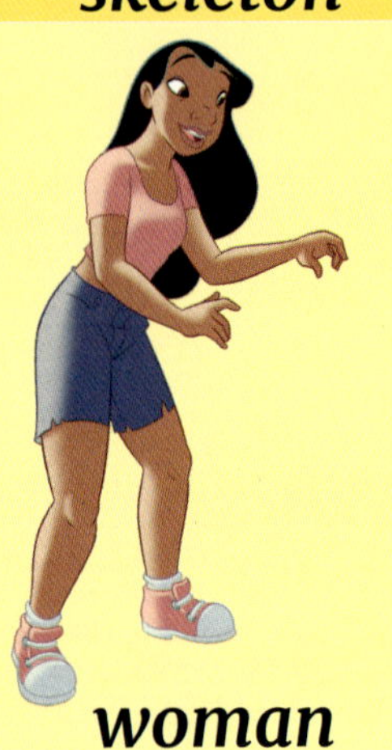

*woman*

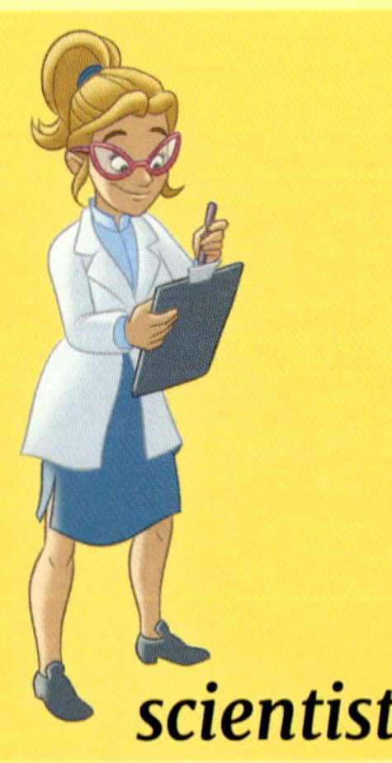

*scientist*

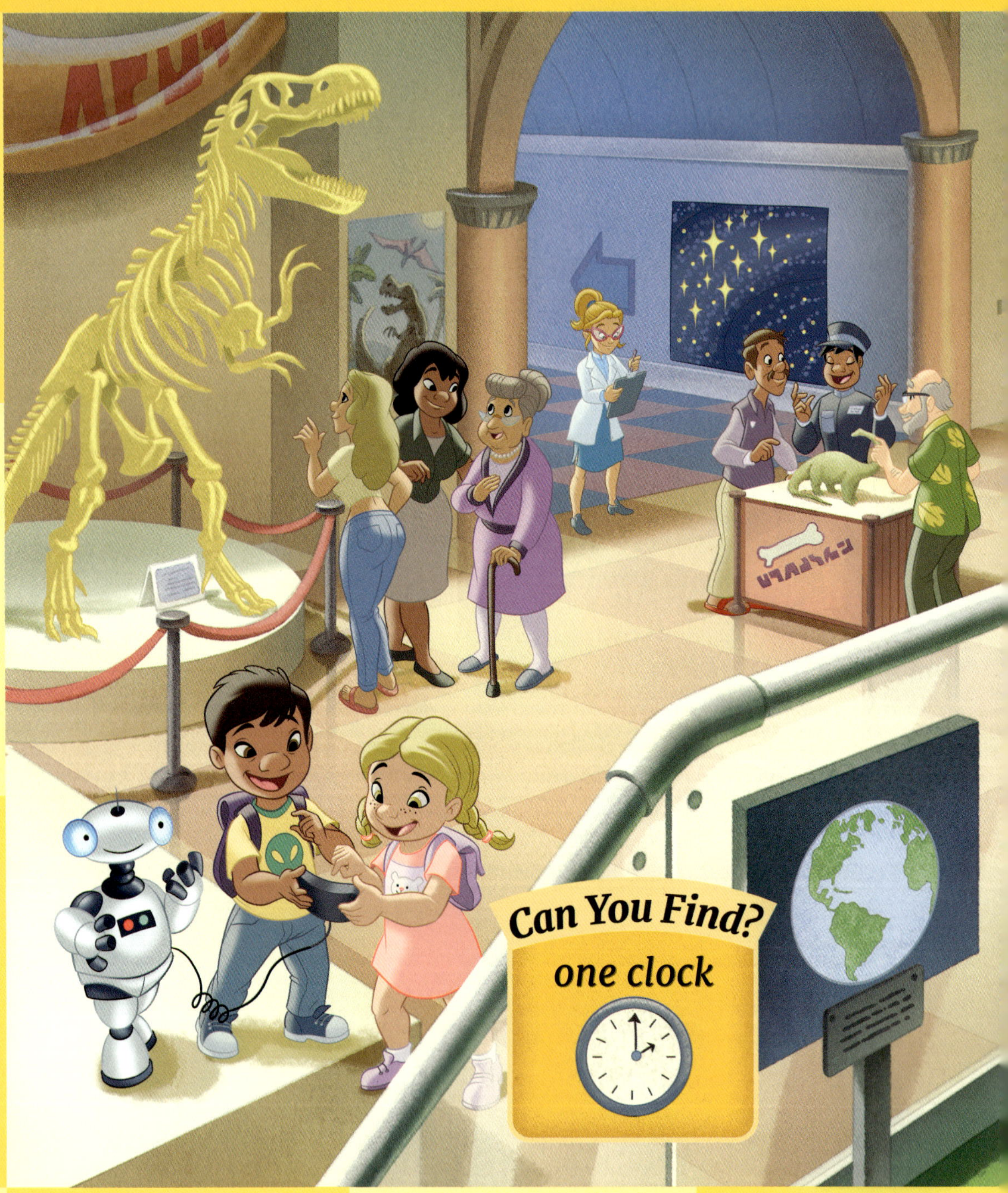

Can You Find?
one clock


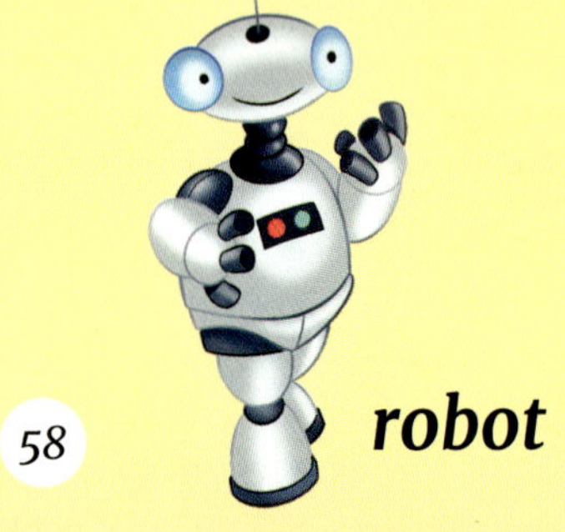

*robot*

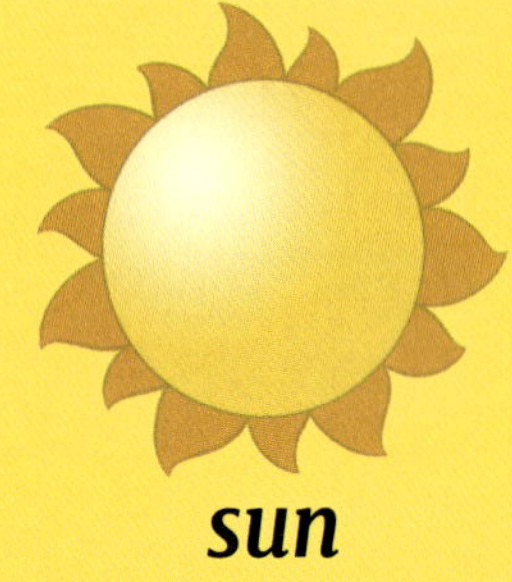

*sun*

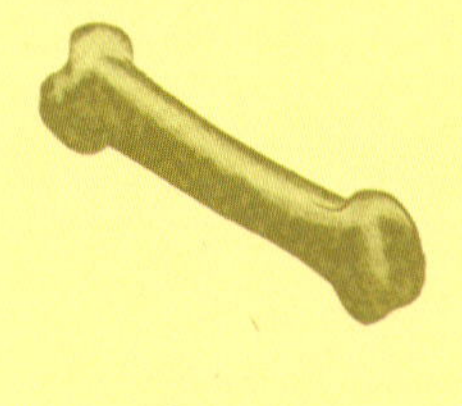

*bone*

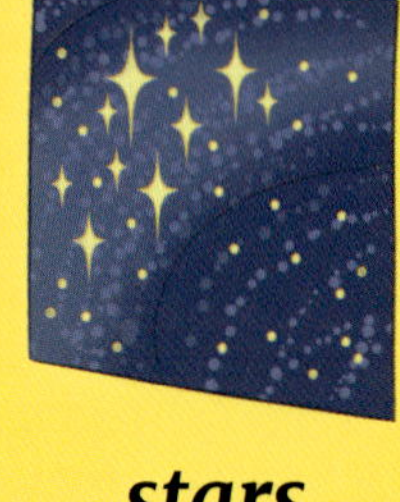

*stars*

men

Earth

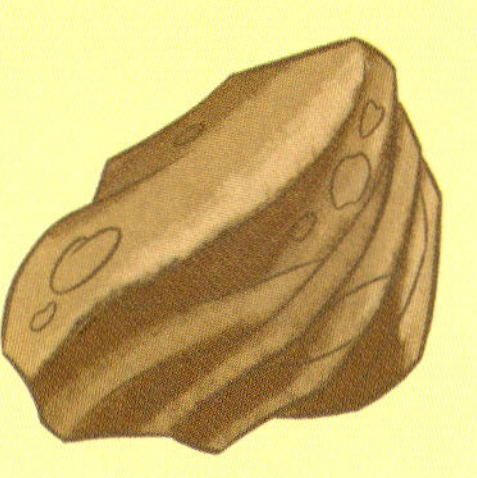

rock

telescope

man

children

space shuttle

moon

women

planets

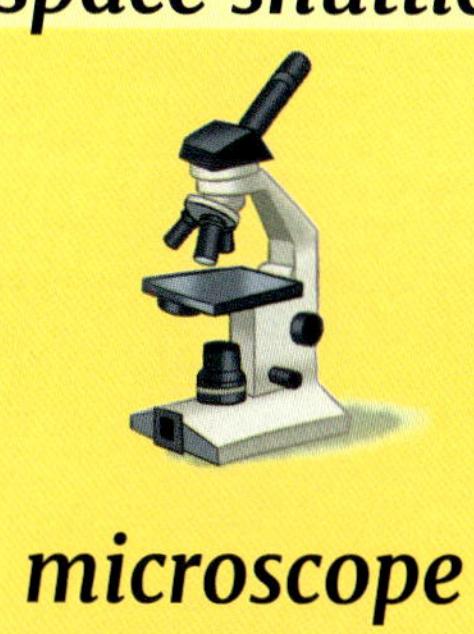

microscope

# Creating Art with Rapunzel

sculpture

paintbrush

ceramics

paper

sketch

paint

artist

pottery

drawing

palette
clay
rag
portrait
art
A day of art is the best day ever!
canvas
painting

# Belle and the Beast Enjoy a Day of Reading

sword

land

globe

rain

magic

bookmark

fairy

dragon

atlas

mountain

books

Can You Find?

Mrs Potts and Chip

sails

sea

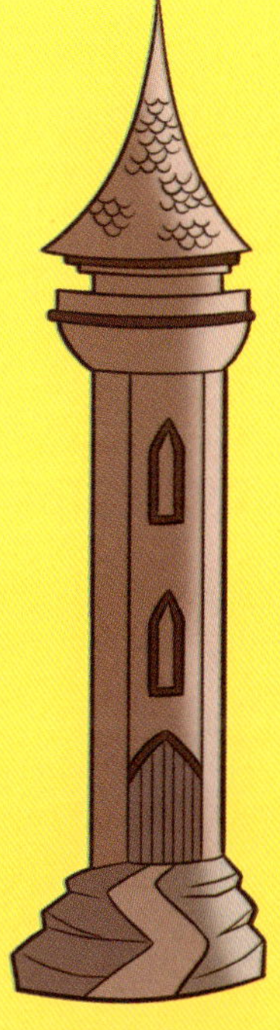

valley

ghost

storybook

tower

# A Concert with Ariel and Sebastian

bass

drum

trombone

saxophone

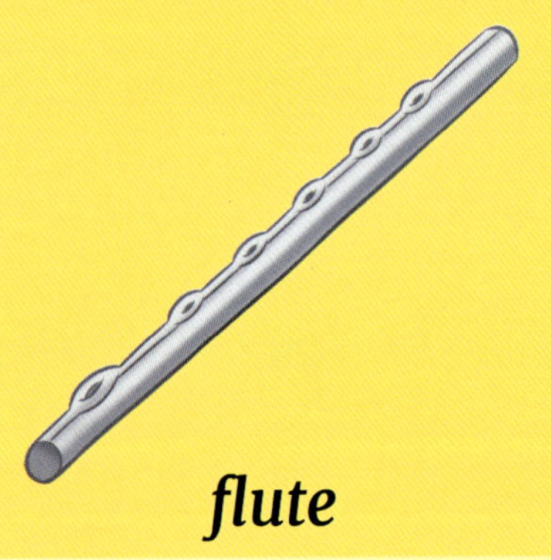

flute

tuba

xylophone

drummer

guitar

musicians

trumpet

harmonica

violin
harp
instruments
tambourine
band
piano
baton
musical notes
Your concerts are always amazing, Sebastian.

# Lilo and Stitch at the Beach

starfish

ocean

sun cream

umbrella

sand

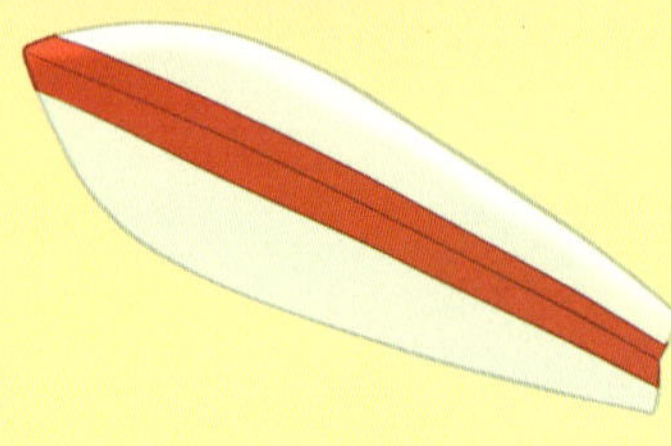

surfboard

sun hat

shell

beach

beach ball

life jacket

beach towel

**Can You Find?**

three shells

seagull

lifeguard

swimsuit

wave

seaweed

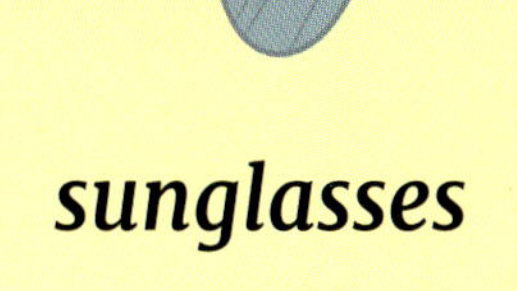
sunglasses

sandcastle

water bottle

# Playing Sports with Mickey and Friends

skiing

football

baseball

basketball

ice skating

ice hockey

tennis

American football

gymnastics

cycling

archery

jogging

roller skating

golf

martial arts

table tennis

snowboarding

swimming

# At the Race with Lightning

crew

fuel

**Can You Find?**

six orange cones

spectators

mud

springs

bolts

nuts

oil can

racers

tyre

ramp

headphones

# Monsters at the Cinema

*movie*

*curtains*

*projector*

*poster*

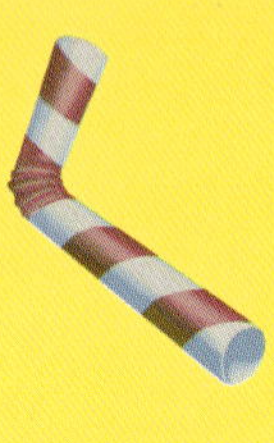

*straw*

*popcorn*

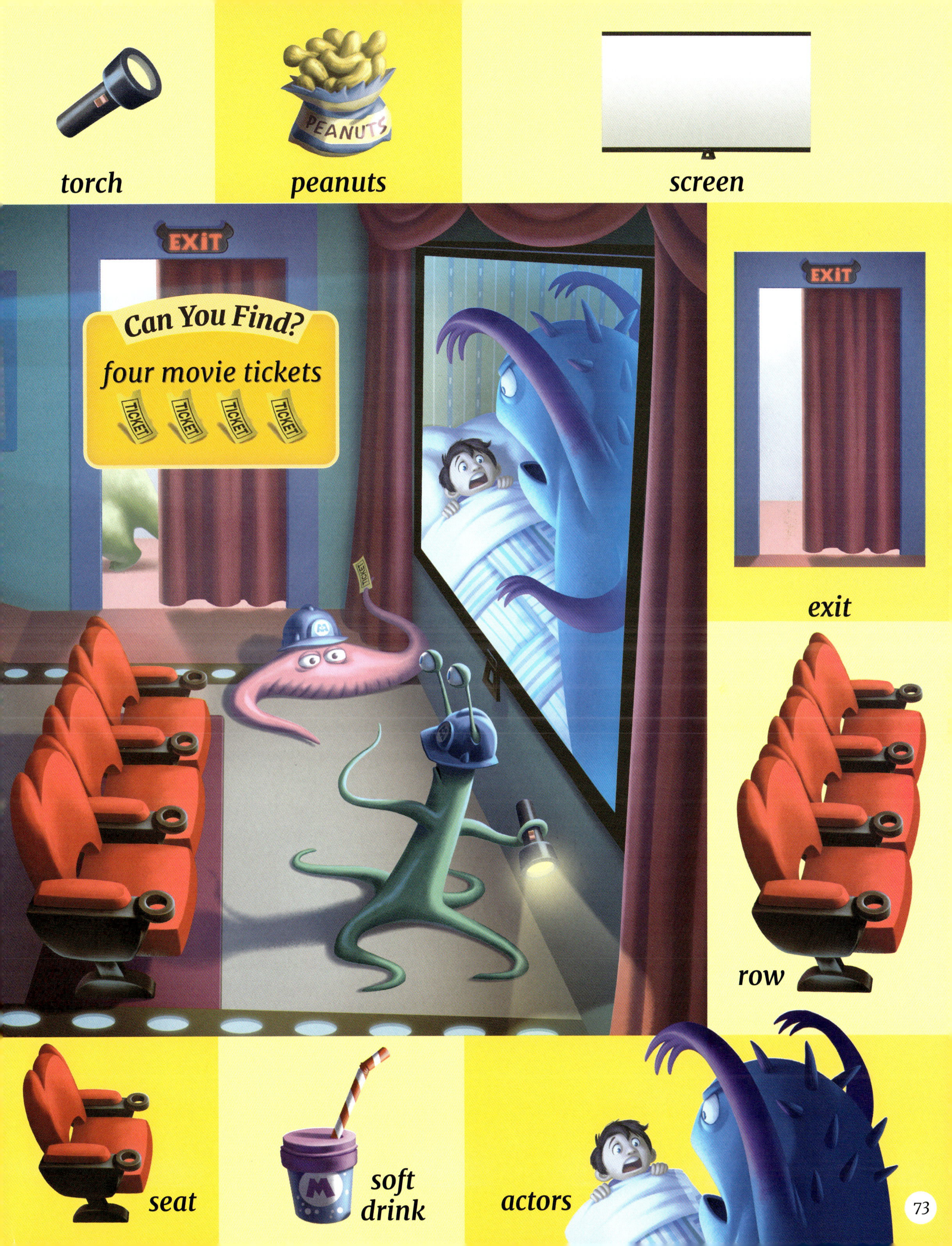

torch

peanuts

screen

EXIT

**Can You Find?**

*four movie tickets*

TICKET TICKET TICKET TICKET

exit

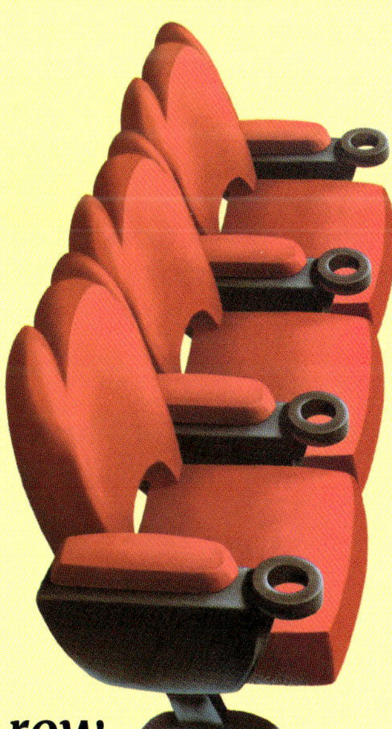

row

seat

soft drink

actors

# A Birthday Party for Anna

balloons

guests

card

candles

cookies

pie

banner

sweets

cupcakes

cake

**Can You Find?**

*three snowflakes*

ribbons

presents

party hat

chocolate

juice

# Belle and the Beast Celebrate Christmas

snowman

wreath

snowflakes

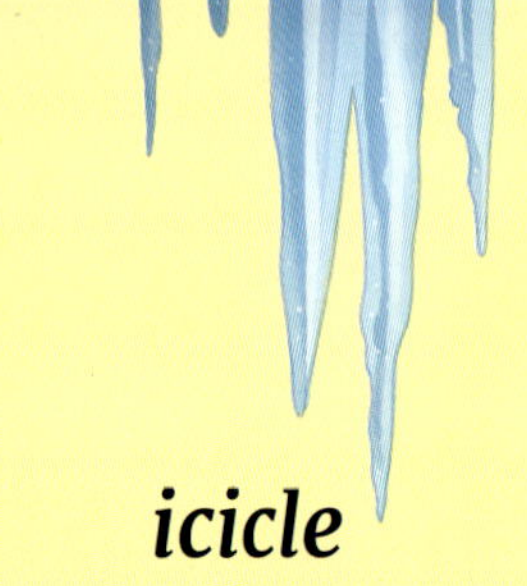

icicle

snowball

angel

holly

handwarmer

ornaments

snow

sledge

## Can You Find?

eight pinecones

Christmas tree

tinsel

Christmas

garland

# All Kinds of Animal Friends!

*What's your favourite animal?*

**Pinocchio's Pets**

**The Aristocats**

**Lady and Tramp's Family**

**Bolt and His Family**

**Pets Are Our Friends**

**Rapunzel's Animal Friends**

# Donald Visits a Farm

bull

hen

chicks

scarecrow

cow

rooster

donkey

lamb

farm

sheep

barn

turkey

horse

calf

goose

colt

**Can You Find?**
seven eggs

duck

goat

pig

hay

# On the Plain with Simba

baboon

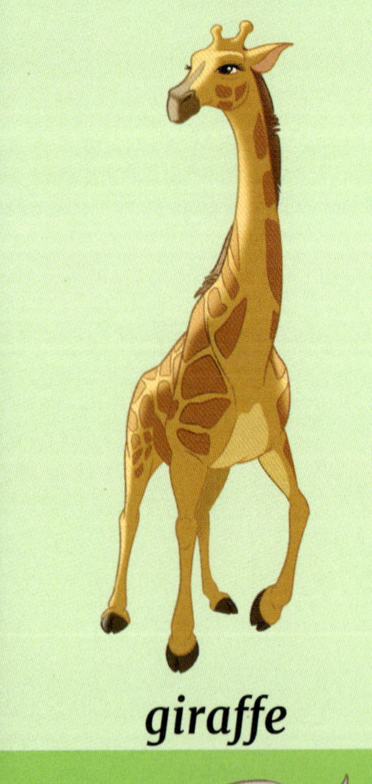
giraffe

hippo

gazelle

cheetah

leopard

hornbill

zebra

gorilla

hyena

## Can You Find?

two of Zazu's loose feathers

lioness

lion

rhino

elephant

wildebeest

lion cub

# In the Jungle with Baloo and Mowgli

bear

monkey

vulture

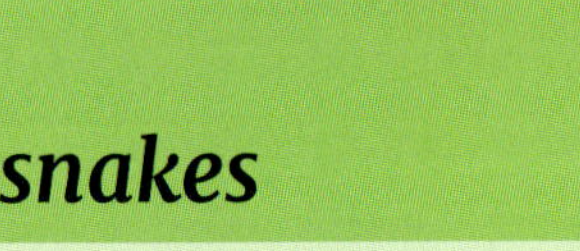

snakes

water buffalo

wolf

panther

crocodile

orangutan

***bat***

***lynx***

***tiger***

*We're having a jungle party!*

***cobra***

***python***

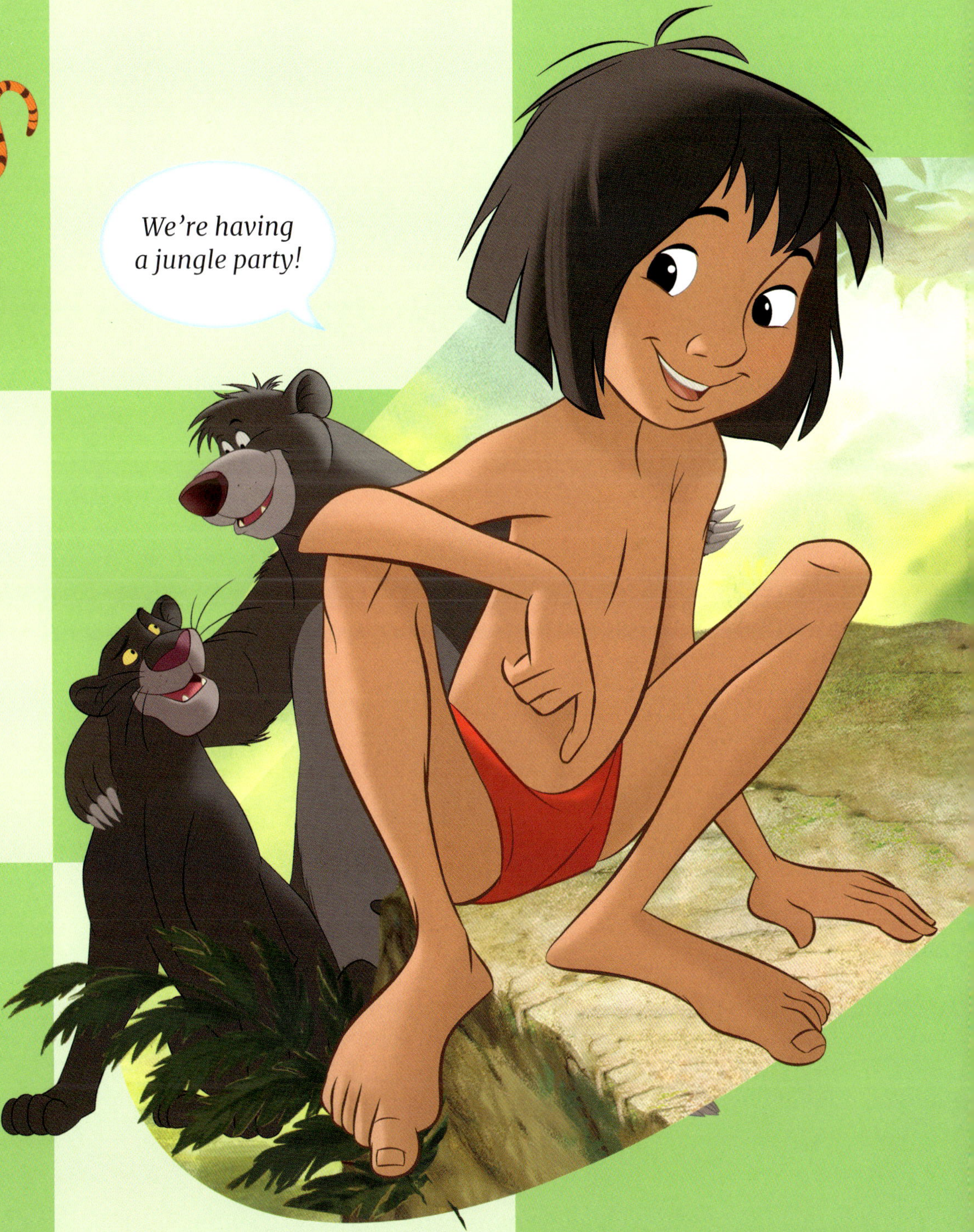

# Russell Goes Bird-Watching

*woodpecker*

*dove*

*hummingbird*

*flamingo*

*crane*

A Wilderness Explorer is a friend to all!

*parrot*

*bluebird*

blue jay
peacock
penguin
puffin
sparrow
swan
ostrich
crow
robin
pigeon
hawk
stork
pelican
toucan
eagle

ANIMALS
and NATURE

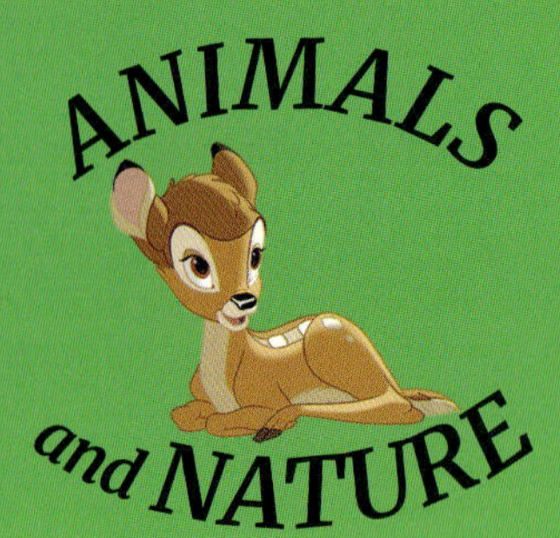

# Bambi's Forest Friends

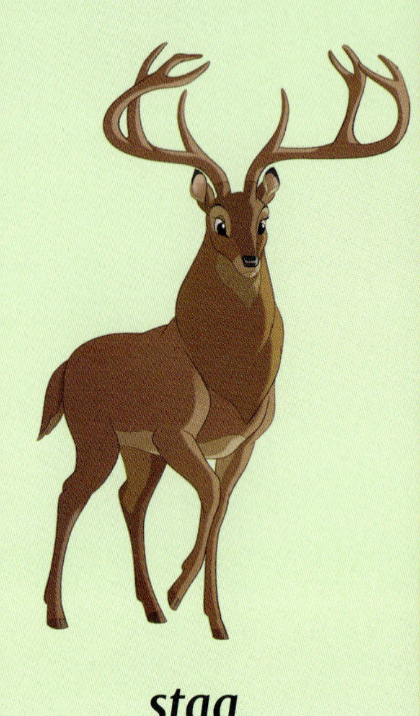

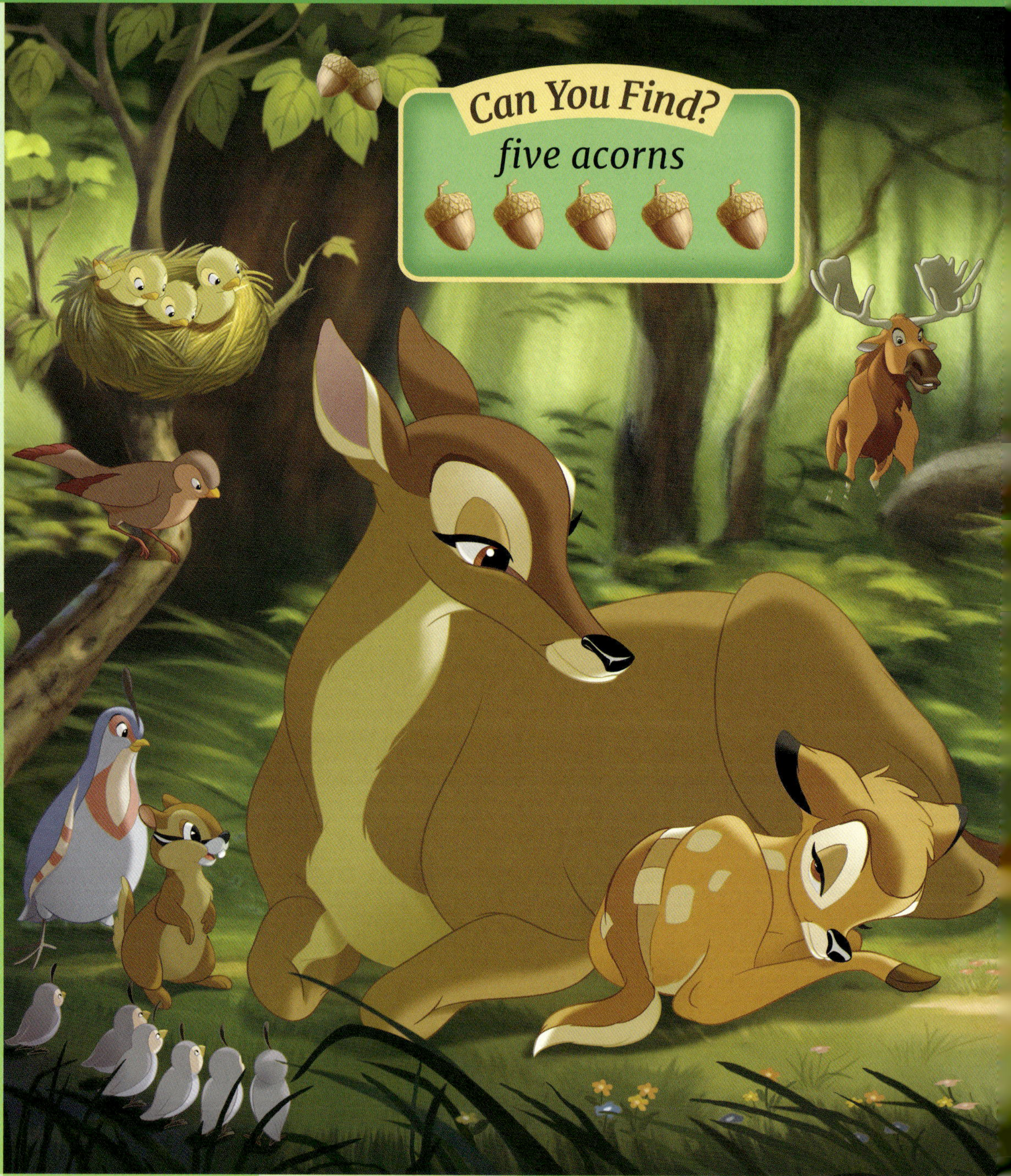
Can You Find?
five acorns

stag

doe

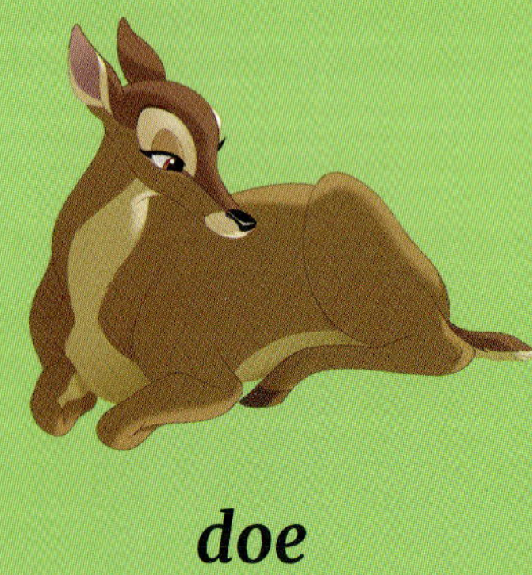

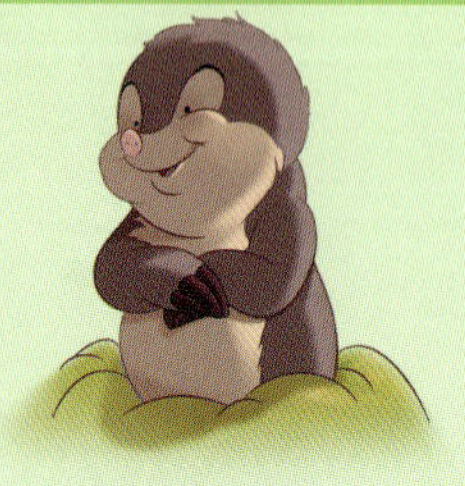

mole

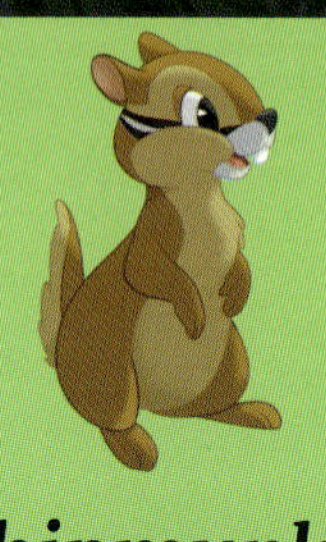

chipmunk

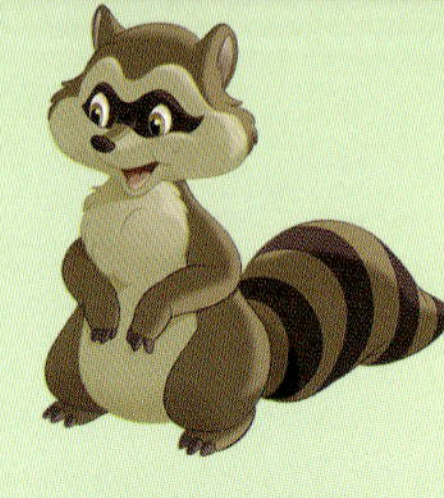

raccoon

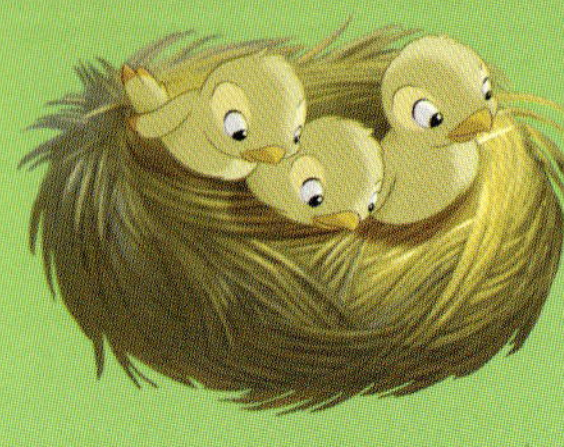

nest

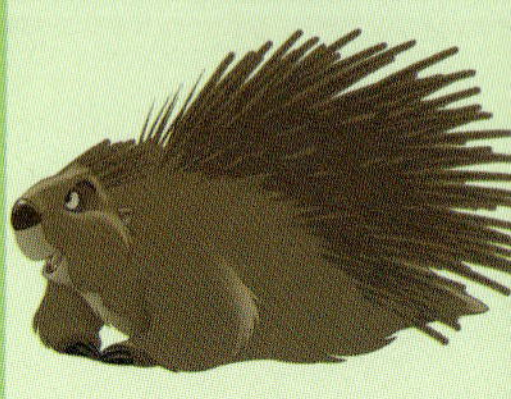

porcupine

badger

fawn

fox

web

squirrel

moose

deer

beaver

skunk

owl

possum

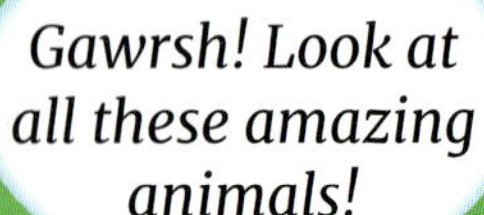


# Goofy's Photo Safari

*Gawrsh! Look at all these amazing animals!*

apes

armadillo

chameleon

camel

coyote

jaguar

kangaroo

koala

manatee

polar bear

reindeer

panda

sloth

walrus

# Nemo and Dory's Ocean World

shark

coral

kelp

clam

ray

otter

starfish

dolphin

sea lion

jellyfish

sea turtles

sea horse

whale
septopus
whale shark
clown fish
crab
Just keep swimming!
squid

# Flik and the World of Bugs

bee

firefly

ladybird

cricket

I've seen all kinds of bugs do great things!

*ant*

*flea*

*tarantula*

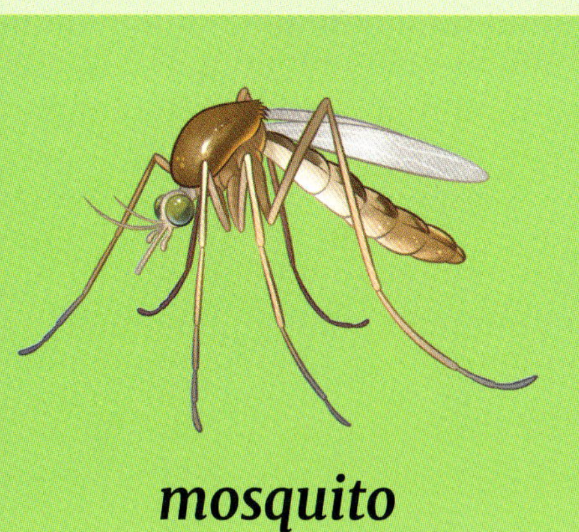
*mosquito*

*hornet*

*moth*

*butterfly*

*dragonfly*

*praying mantis*

*spider*

*fly*

*wasp*

*grasshopper*

*caterpillar*

*beetle*

# Flowers in Wonderland

*daffodil*

*iris*

*lilac*

*pansy*

*bluebells*

*tulip*

*flowers*

*rose*

*lily*

lavender
carnation
violet
daisy
orchid
poppies
sunflower
You can learn a lot of things from the flowers!

# An Adventure with Elsa and Anna

shadow

trail

waterfall

bark

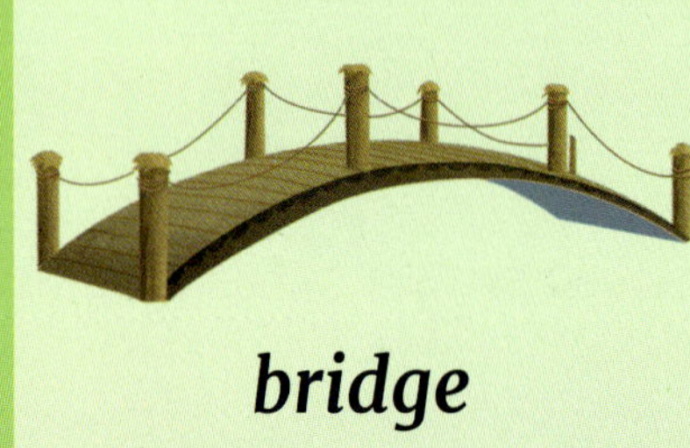

bridge

sky

cave

rainbow

roots

hole

branch

trees

mountain

## Can You Find?

six butterflies

leaf

river

cloud

sun

# Peter Pan's Camping Trip

**Can You Find?**

two pairs of yellow eyes hidden in the bushes

bait

forest

campfire

log

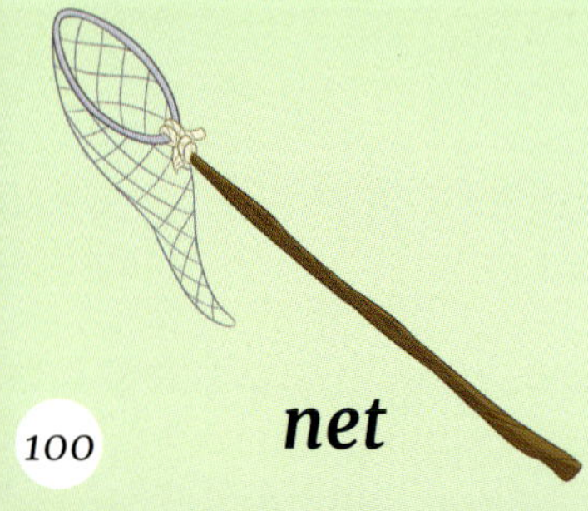

net

beehive

grass

marshmallows

bushes

feather
stones
smoke
rope
moon
bats
picnic basket
sleeping bag
tent
sticks
stars
lantern
fishing rod

# Pinocchio Becomes a Real Boy

hip
shoulder
head
hands
hair
eyebrows
eyelashes
eyes
ear
cheek
nose
chin
wrist
waist
ankle
thigh
body
leg
feet

# All Kinds of Feelings

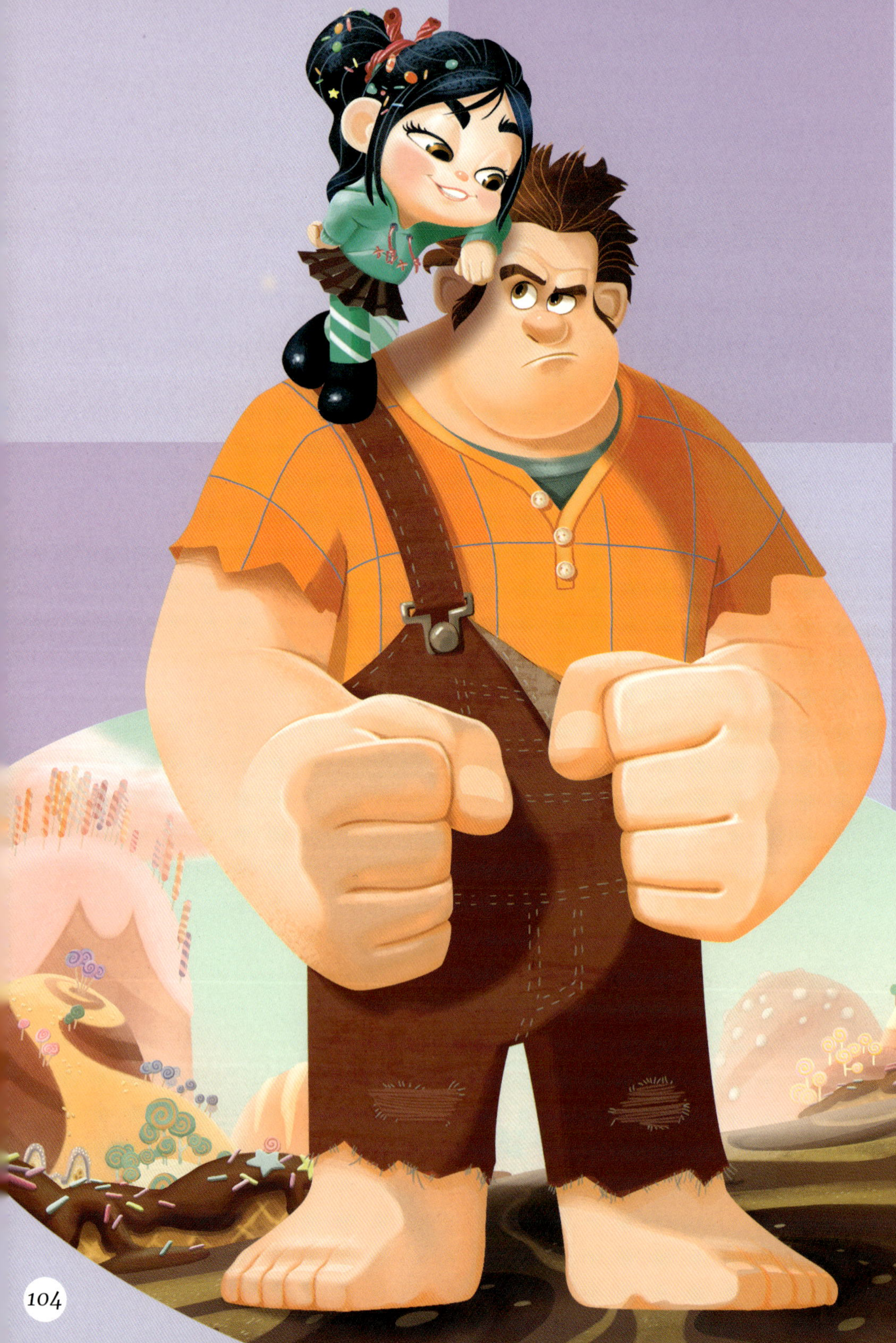

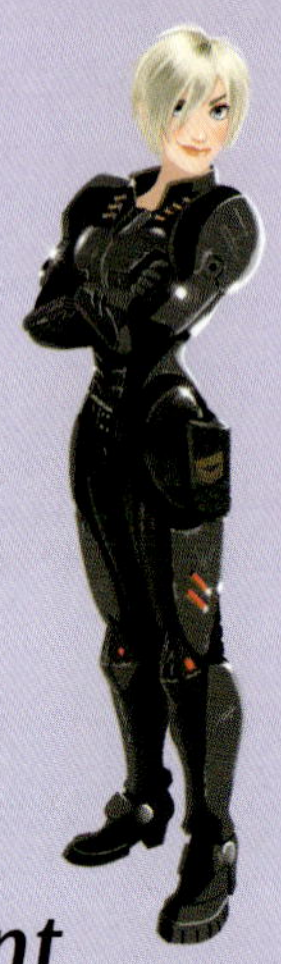

confident

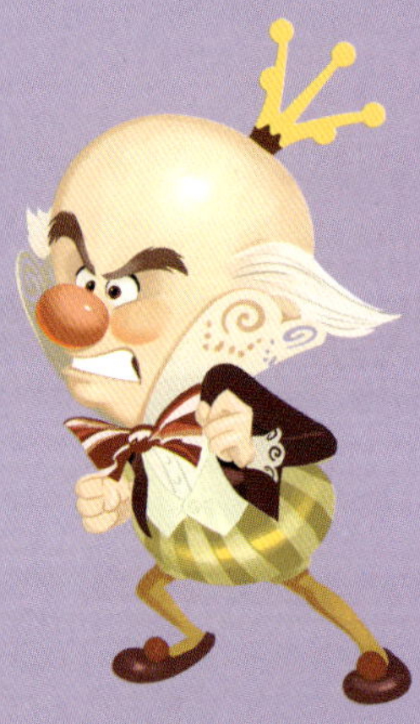

angry

curious

nervous

proud

shy

silly

surprised

confused

scared

sleepy

sad

happy

excited

# A Busy Year for Princesses

January

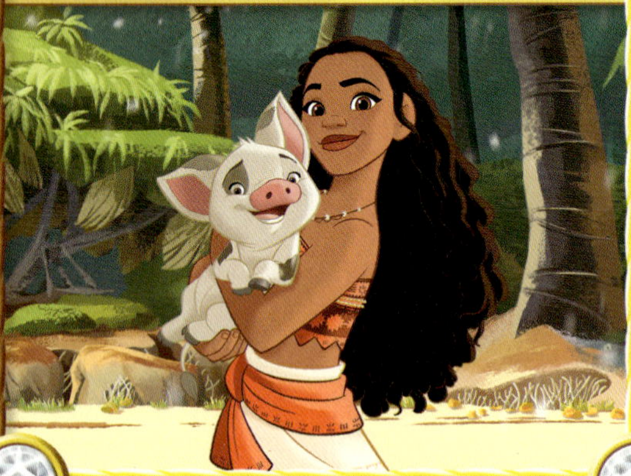

February

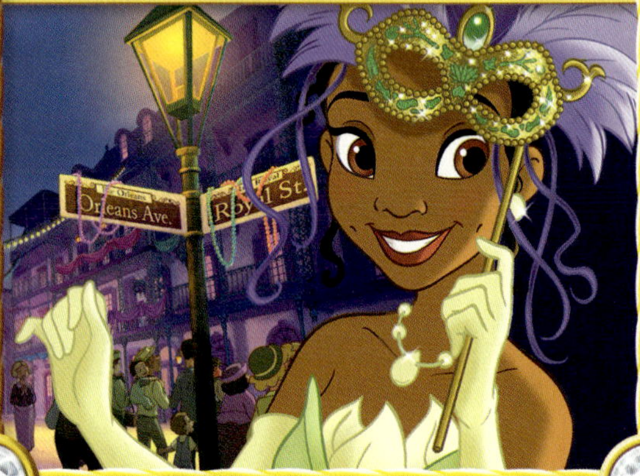

March

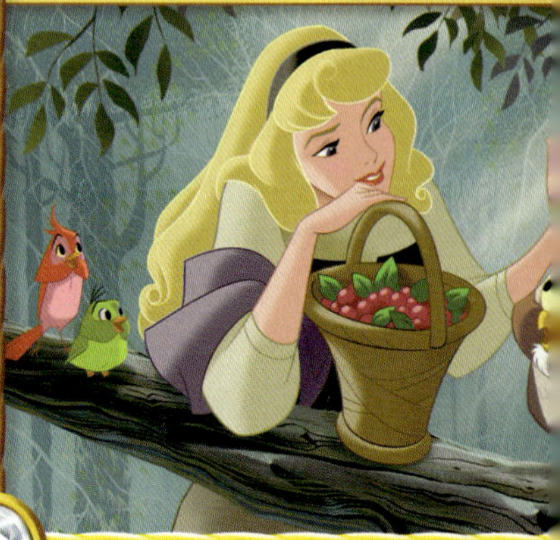

May

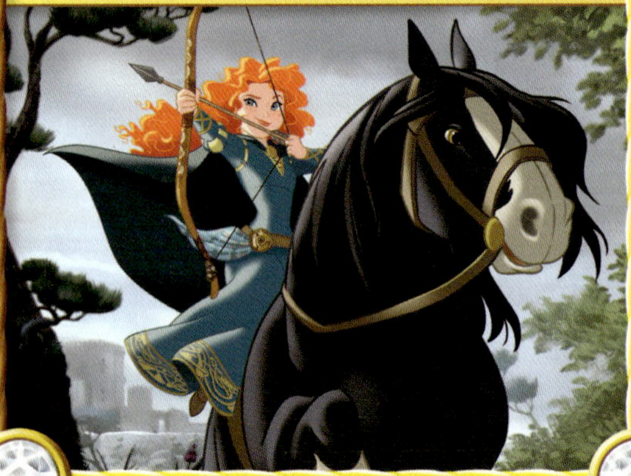

June

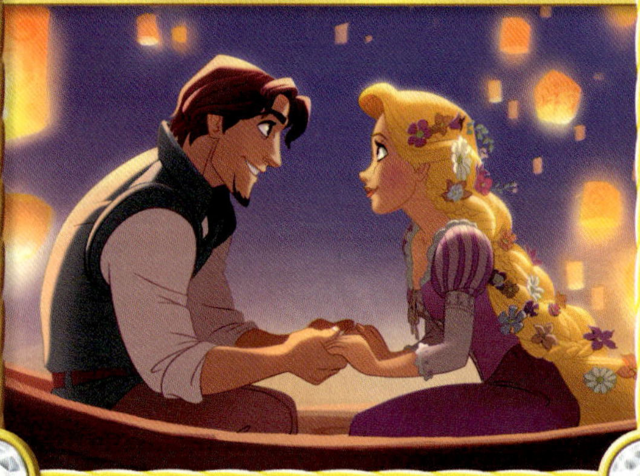

July

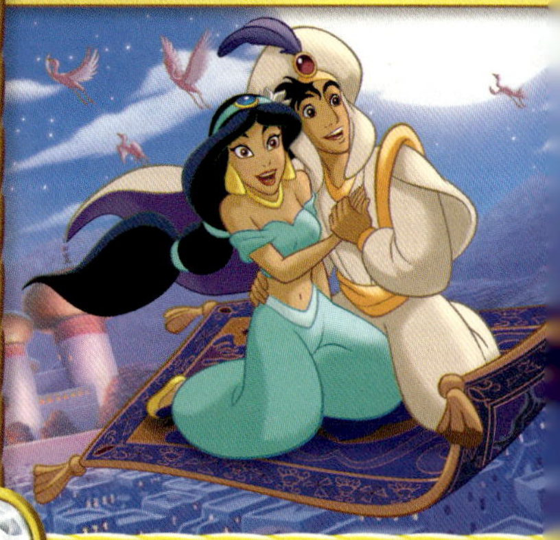

September

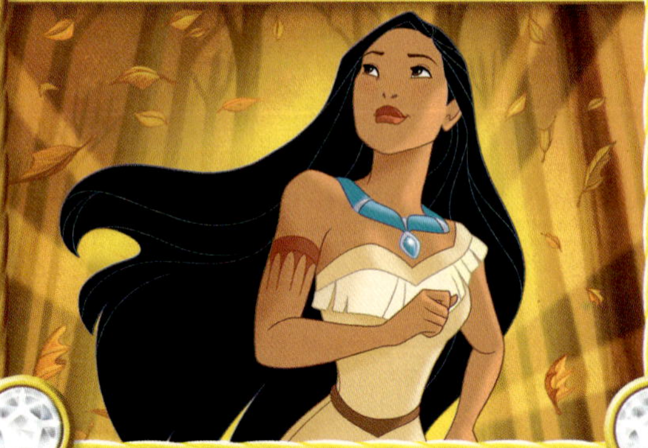

October

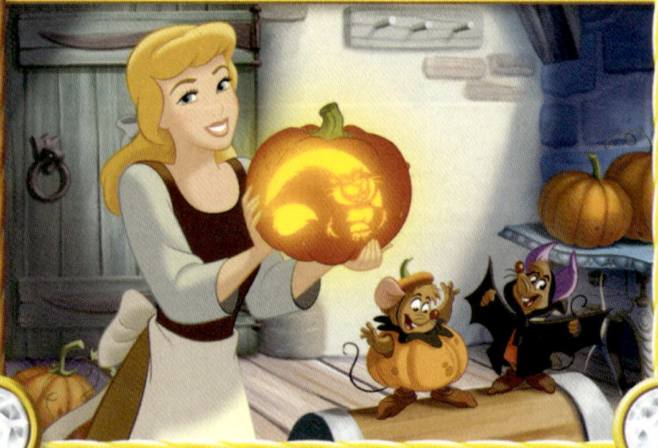

November

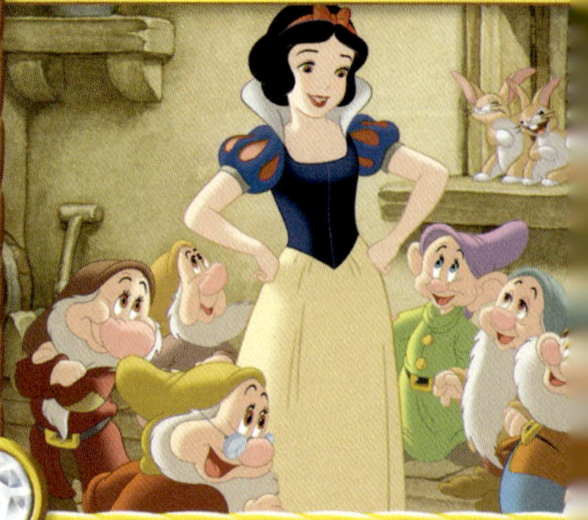

April

August

December

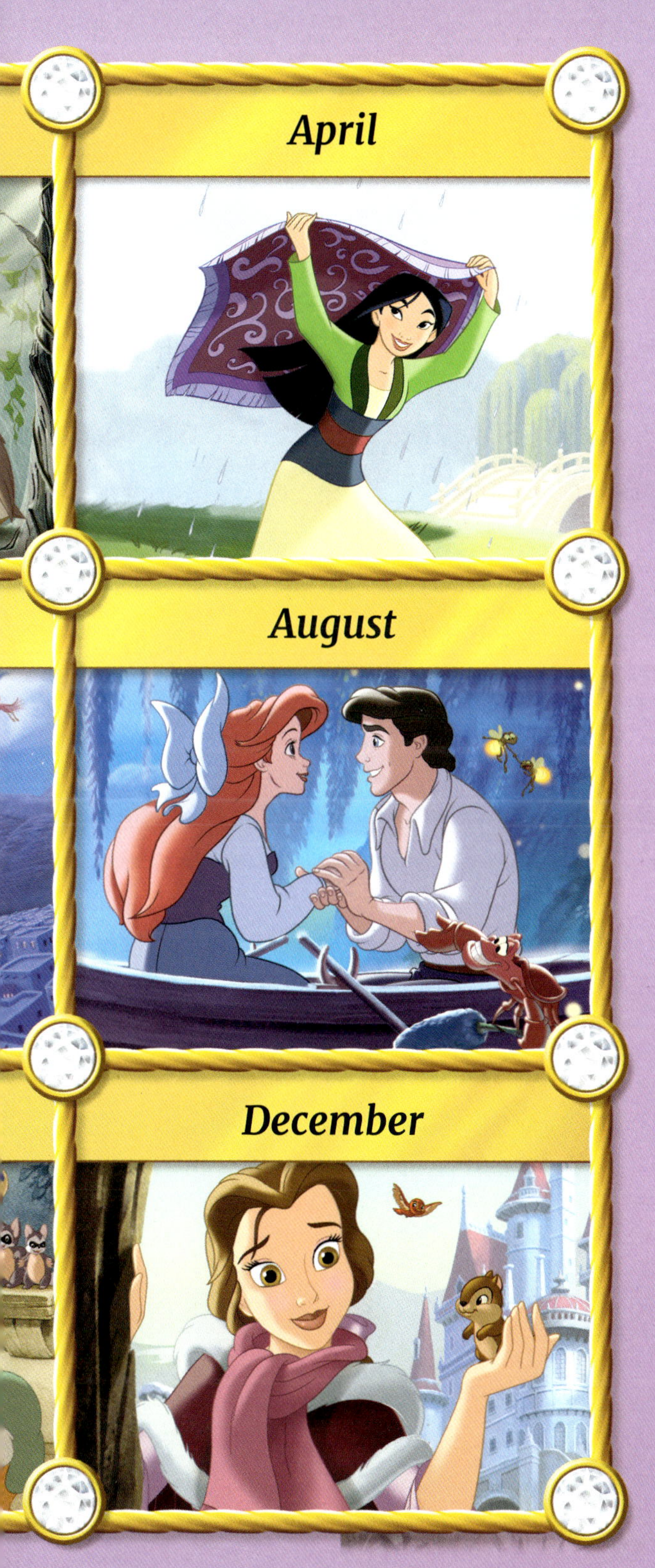

# Seasons

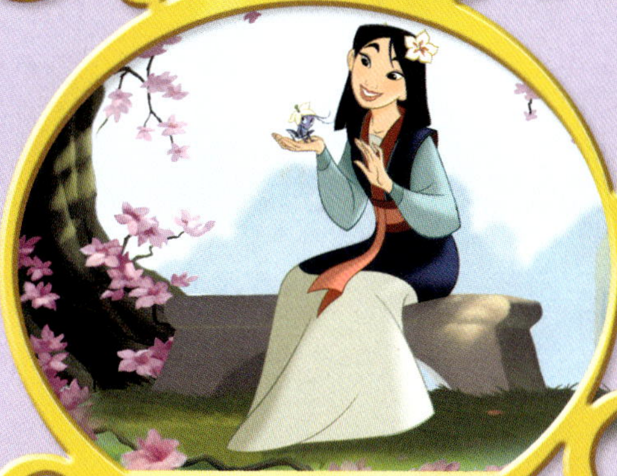

spring

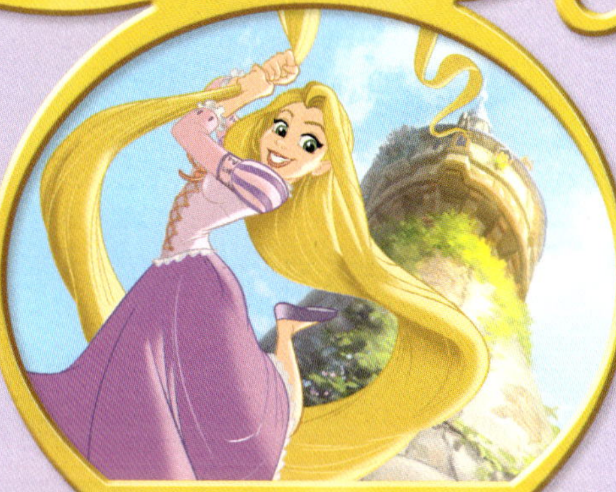

summer

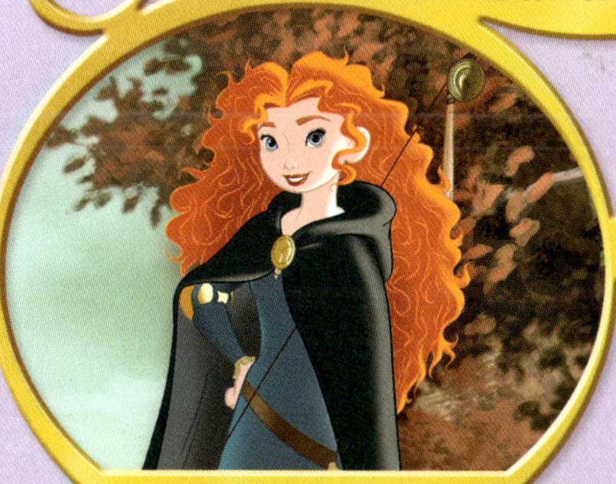

autumn

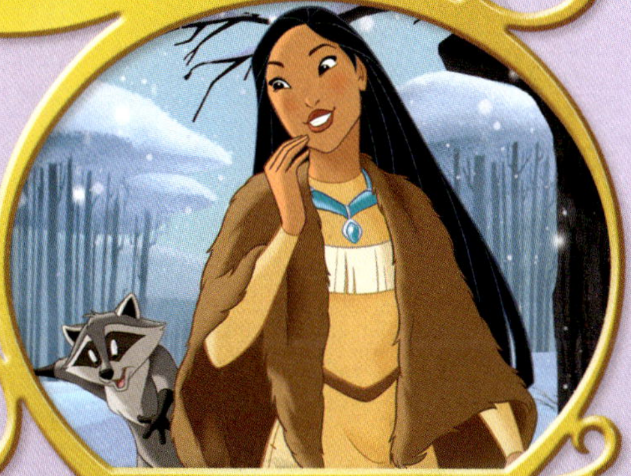

winter

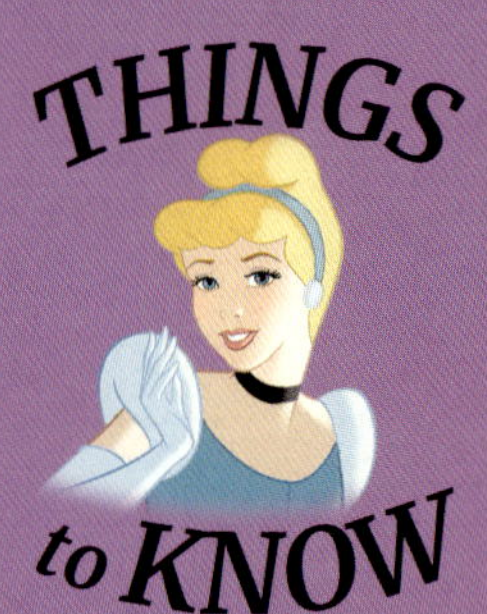


# Spending Time with Cinderella

morning

noon

afternoon

night

midnight

# Days of the Week

# How Many Dalmatians?

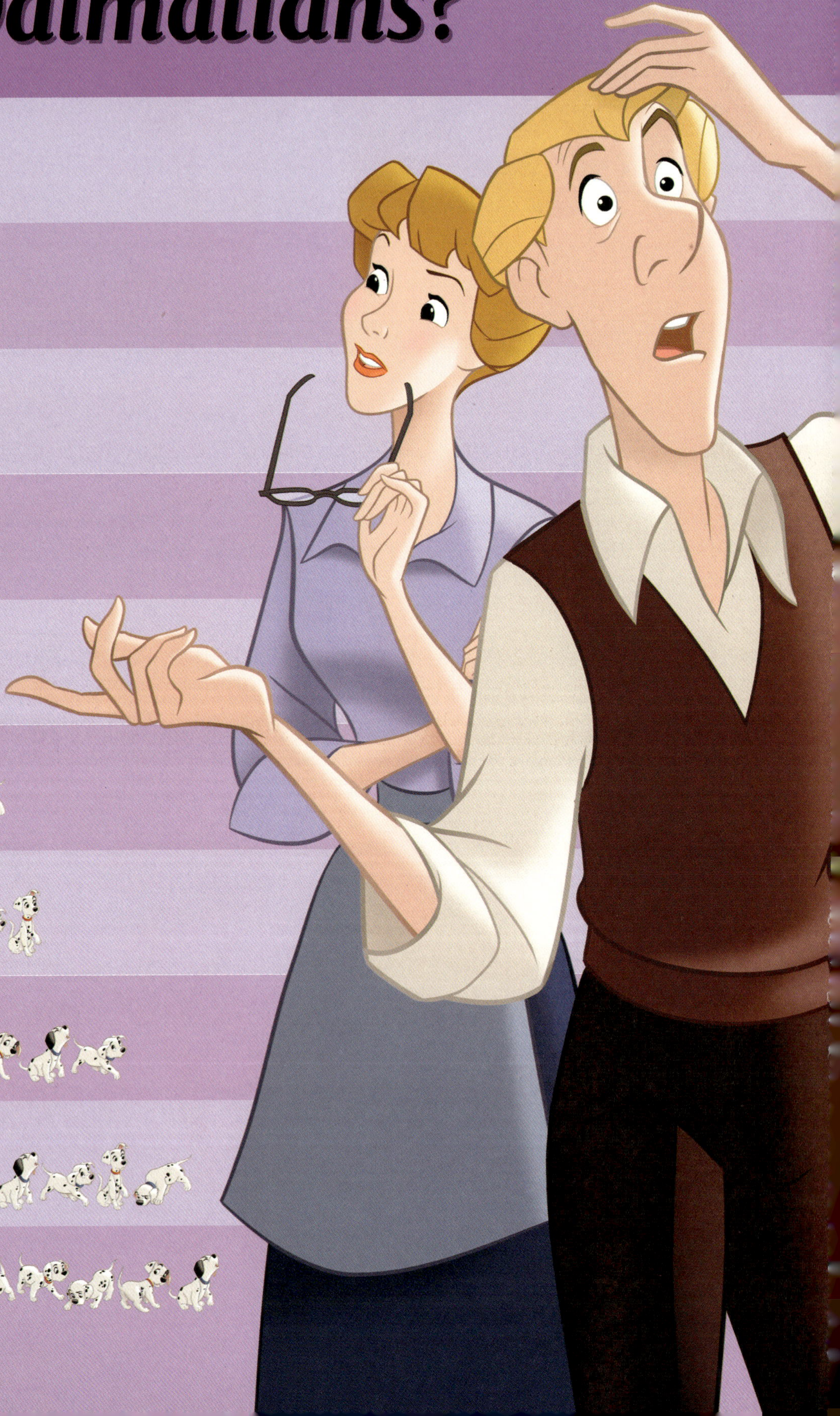

0 zero

1 one

2 two

3 three

4 four

5 five

6 six

7 seven

8 eight

9 nine

How many puppies are there?

10 ten

11 eleven

12 twelve

13 thirteen

14 fourteen

15 fifteen

16 sixteen

17 seventeen

18 eighteen

19 nineteen

20 twenty

# Finding Shapes in Wonderland

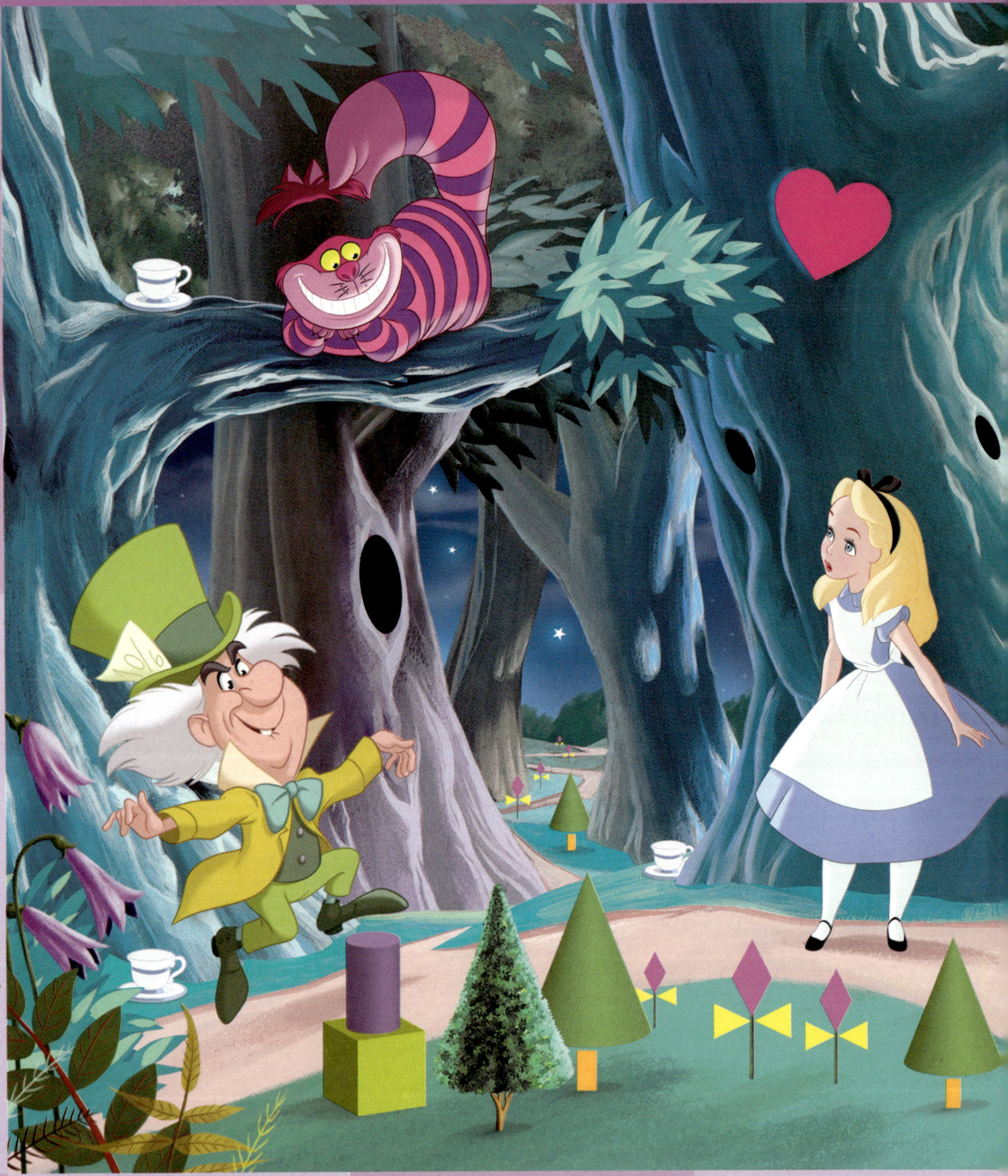

*oval*

*cylinder*

*circle*

*square*

*rectangle*

*heart*

Can You Find?
four teacups
cone
diamond
star
crescent
cube
triangle

# Cars of All Colours

*red*

*yellow*

*orange*

*green*

grey

white

black

3 BOOTH

brown

Can You Find?

seven paintbrushes

pink

blue

purple

# Olaf's Favourite Opposites

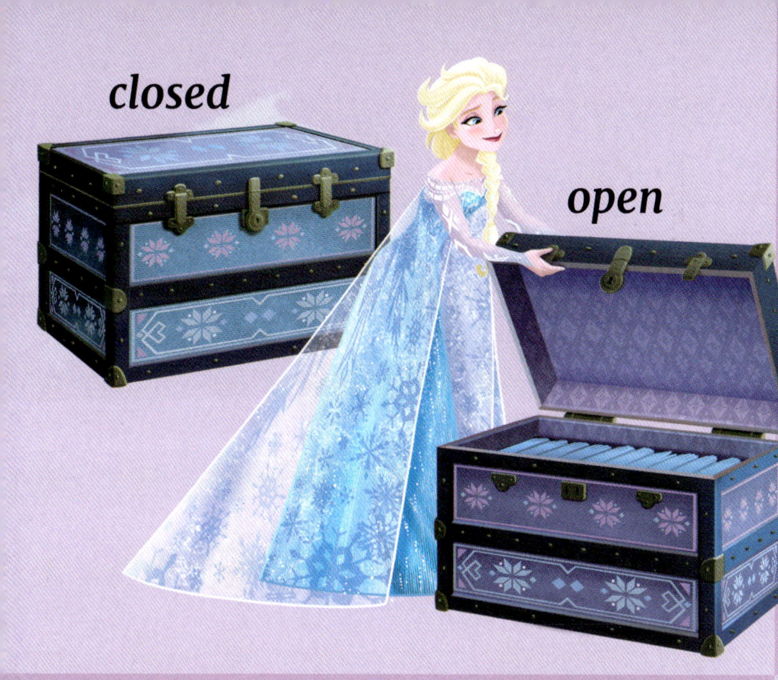
closed
open

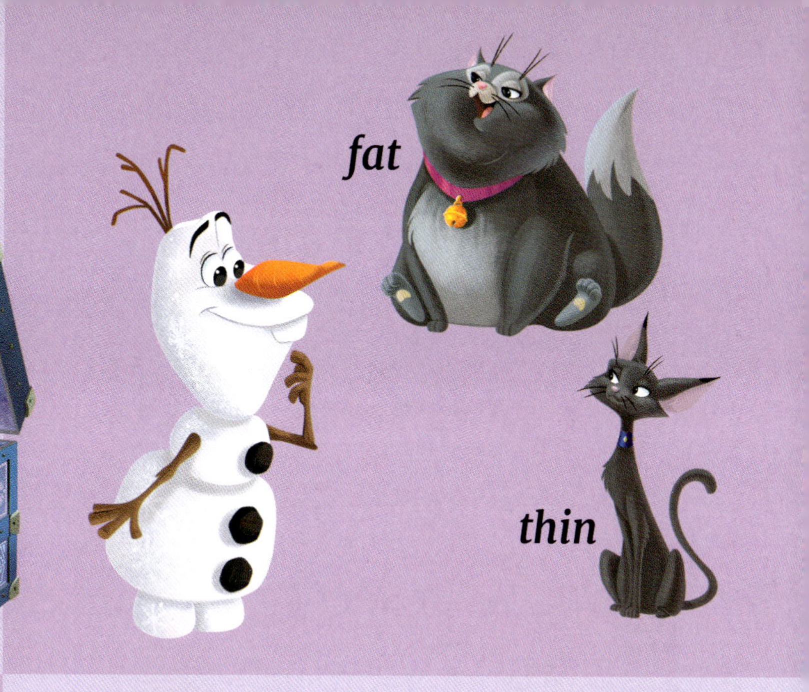
fat
thin

bad
good

dry
wet

loud
quiet

cold
hot

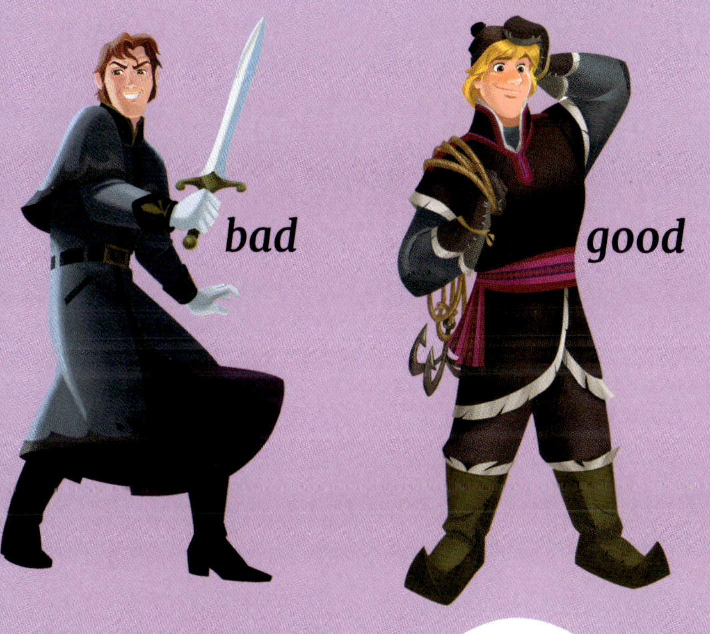

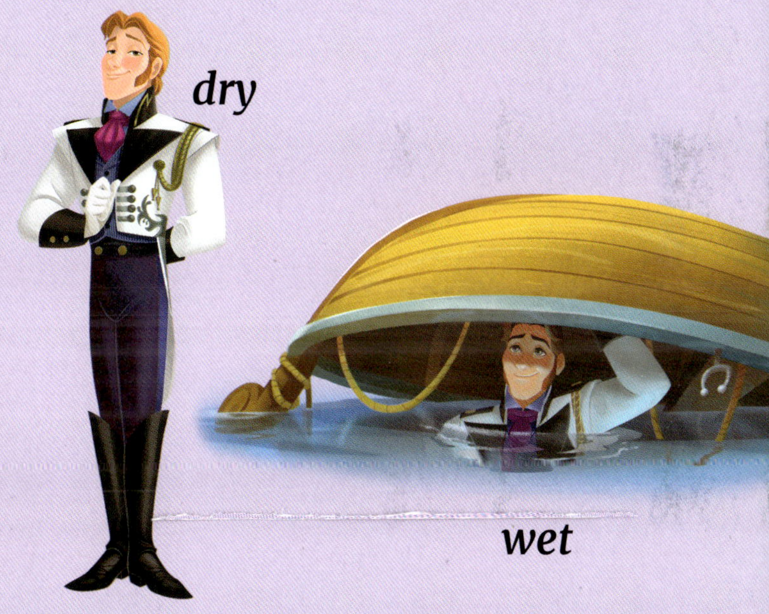

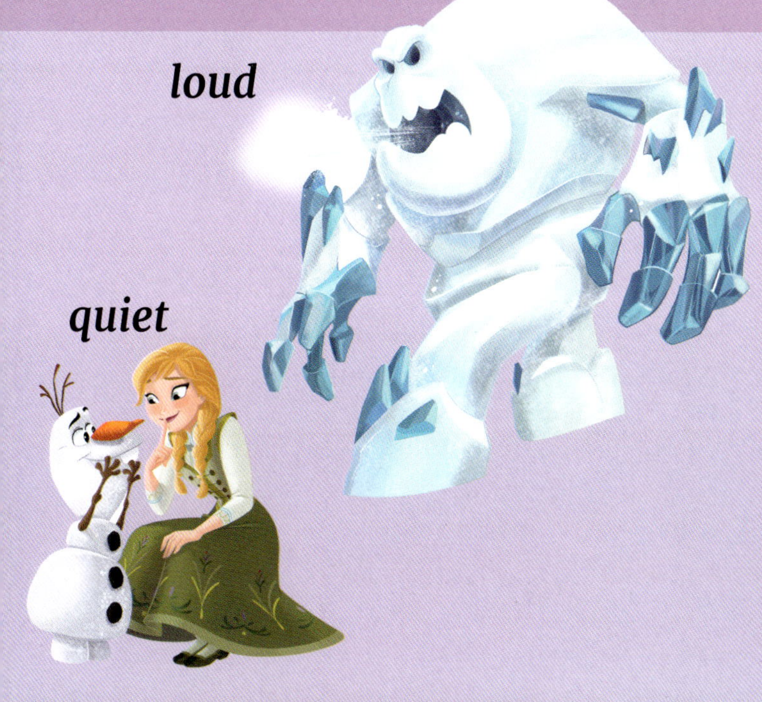

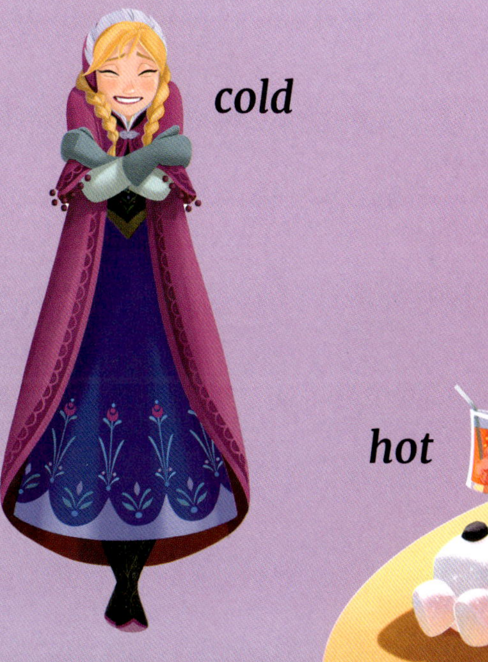

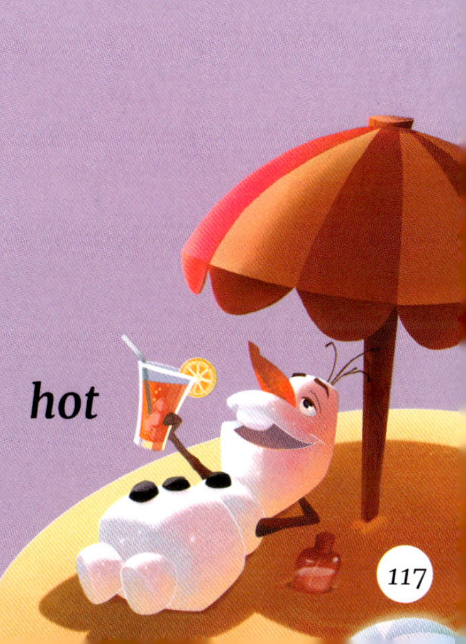

# Busy Belle, Busy Beast

sing

talk

clean

stand

write

jump

kiss

smile

read

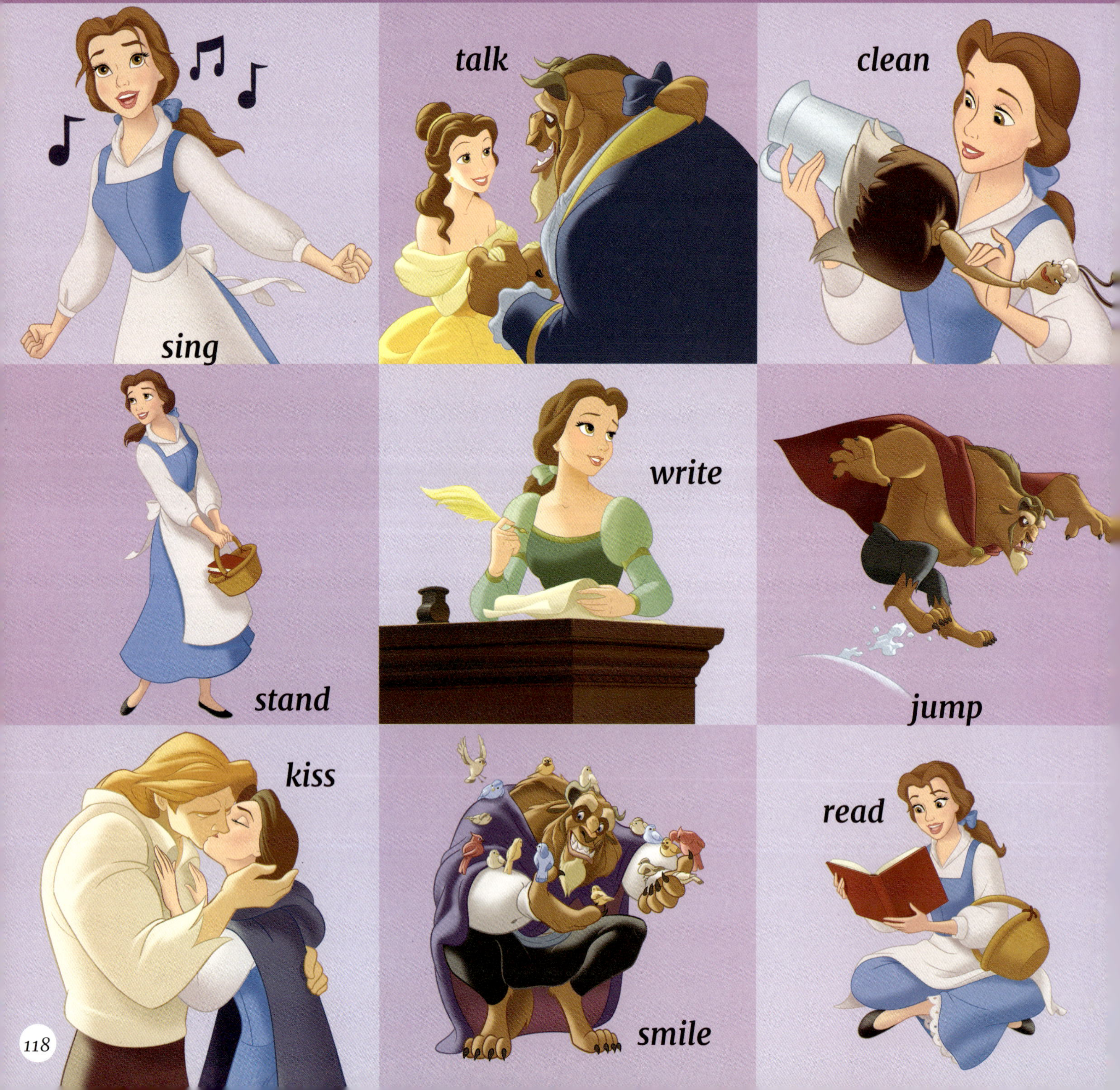

whisper
listen
think
sleep
laugh
dance
drink
sit
build
eat
run
wake up

# Simba and Nala Play in the Pride Lands

through

behind
in front of

around

over
under

on
off

in
out

Kristoff

Ralph

Pinocchio

Aurora

Peter Pan

Vanellope

Alice

Bambi

Scuttle

Zazu

Jasmine

Flounder

Felix

Lady

Timothy

Sven